Henry Sutton was born in Norfolk in 1963. He is a journalist and travel writer and the author of five previous novels, *Gorleston*, *Bank Holiday Monday*, *The Househunter*, *Flying*, and *Kids' Stuff*, also published by Serpent's Tail. In 2002 he won an Arts Council of England Writers' Award. He lives in South London.

Praise for *Kids' Stuff*

'. . . this intense tale explores family dysfunction and history's nasty habit of repeating itself' *Daily Mirror*

'It is Sutton's greatest achievement here that his narrative keeps us interested in the fate of such a profoundly unpleasant man. This fascination may be unhealthy, even upsetting, but it is expertly managed by acutely observed dialogue and almost forensic description . . . Countless writers, sociologists and confessional television shows mostly fail to help us to a better understanding of how people can do unspeakable things to each other. Henry Sutton succeeds without even posing the question' *Times Literary Supplement*

'Henry Sutton has taken us into one man's Hell and made it seem frighteningly real' *Sunday Telegraph*

'The points which Sutton wants to convey about modern masculinity seem to benefit from the complete awfulness of the person putting them into practice . . . *Kids' Stuff* succeeds . . . through the sheeer vigour of its conception' *Guardian*

‘As an exploration of the fruitlessness of trying to placate the past, this book is powerful and distressing’ *Independent on Sunday*

‘Sutton is a good writer . . . gutsy, muscular. This is a no-nonsense account of one man’s losing battle to keep the disparate strands of his life from unravelling’ *Time Out*

‘Distinctly urban tale of failed relationships and family dysfunction . . . With voyeuristic intensity, he lovingly ropes us into their little corner of domestic hell’ *Independent*

‘What Sutton does so well here is render the blank landscape of portacabins and deserted car parks as atmospheric and menacing as any urban “mean street”. Sutton’s subtle but wholly gripping account of Marks’ passage from knocking up shelves to the brink of murder is entirely, disturbingly, convincing.’ *Big Issue in the North*

‘Henry Sutton’s new novel is about a lot of thrings: the ugliness of modern life, the silent griefs we all carry with us, and that ever-fragile frontier between love and hate. But it is also a compelling, unnerving journey into those darker recesses of the mind that we all keep well-hidden from public view. It’s a remarkable novel – spare, uncompromising, deeply felt. And it’s a reminder – as if one is needed – that Henry Sutton is a terrific writer’ Douglas Kennedy

Thong Nation

Henry Sutton

A complete catalogue record for this book can be obtained from the British Library on request

First published in 2005 by Serpent's Tail,
4 Blackstock Mews, London N4 2BT
website: www.serpentstail.com

Printed by Mackays of Chatham, plc

10 9 8 7 6 5 4 3 2 1

Part One
Splendour, Debenhams, £15

Majorcan Dreams

'Hi! Can everybody hear me at the back? No? Yes? Okey-dokey. My name's Zara and I'll be looking after you while you're on the island. So I hope you're not going to be too naughty.'

I always say this and the punters always laugh and, yes, invariably they are incredibly naughty. They get smashed and start fighting. They shag their best mates' girlfriends. Some of them get to shag me behind their girlfriends' backs, behind Pedro's back.

Pedro's my current fella. He runs the Autos Serra car-hire franchise in Alcudia. And he has a thick Spanish cock. It's not the longest cock I've ever encountered, but it's certainly the thickest, which is sort of odd because Pedro is tall and skinny, for a Spaniard.

I can't believe I'm thinking about Pedro's cock while I'm sitting here at the front of the coach with sixty-eight punters in the back, as the coach pulls out of Palma Airport en route for the Hotel Gran Sol, Las Gaviotas, Alcudia, which is in the north-east of the island, some fifty minutes away. Plus it's only 6.45 a.m. It's not fully light. Judging by the smell of alcohol on their breath, their bloodshot eyes and the way they struggled aboard the coach, most of my punters are still pissed from last night. They were delayed at Manchester for four hours and had to wait another hour and a half at the airport in Majorca because their luggage was sent to the wrong carousel, in the wrong terminal building. It happens every time.

The bigger tour operators like JMC and Thomson never seem to suffer such problems. But the company I work for doesn't have much clout with the baggage handlers. In fact, we're like the lowest of the low on the island, except in one department. We have the best-looking reps. We're all dead fucking gorgeous, especially me. I'm five-three, have a thirty-four-inch, DD bust, blue eyes and a yard of bottle-blonde hair, which drives Spanish men nuts, without fail.

Take Miguel, the coach driver today: he can't keep his eyes off me. I would tell him to keep his eyes on the road, but I don't want to reprimand him in front of the punters. Besides, I like to be noticed, whatever the time of day. He's also making me feel rather hot and tingly. Or perhaps that's just because I can't stop thinking about Pedro's stubby cock – rolling back his smelly foreskin and sucking the bulbous end into my mouth, so it's like I'm chewing a squash ball. A squash ball with a split in it.

Looking over my shoulder, I notice there's this complete hunk sitting just behind Miguel – brown eyes, black hair and deep tan already. How come I missed him earlier? And the fact that he appears to be on his own? The way I'm feeling right now I wouldn't be surprised if I found myself burying my head in his lap before we hit Inca (which is about halfway to Alcudia, bang in the middle of the island). I'm pretty experienced at giving guys blow jobs on buses. I used to do it on the way to school.

I turn back to face the road, through the giant windscreen, wondering what it is with me and this job, and sex. Kim has this idea it's to do with the sun and being reps, like we're in charge, we're in power – and, wow, do the punters look up to us. It might be a cliché, but it's sort of true.

Kim's my best friend out here – she works in the Hotel Regina, also in Las Gaviotas – and so far she's shagged two more men than me since the season started. I'm determined to even things up by the end of August, despite wanting to hang on to Pedro – you might have some idea why by now. And guess what? I already know who's going to be the next lucky fella.

'Before you lot nod off,' I say, having picked up the dicky mike (they're always dicky), 'I'd just like to tell you a little bit about how we organise things at Majorcan Dreams, what to expect at the resort, and how – are you all listening at the back? – we guarantee that you have the holiday of a lifetime.'

I can recite this spiel without even thinking about it, on automatic. The thing about being a rep, as Kim keeps pointing out, is the repetition. Kim's on her third season. I was a virgin when I came out in early April. Well, not a virgin virgin, of course, but a virgin to this business. Which is perhaps why, it suddenly occurs to me, Kim's two up. She knows the ins and outs better than anyone, those tucked-away places in Las Gaviotas which are perfect for a quickie. Still, I haven't done too badly – I'm not going to reveal my total so far, I'm far too modest, but I will tell you about the first punter I shagged. I'm particularly proud of that one.

He was called Warren, and Warren was here with his girlfriend and another couple. They were all from Stockport or somewhere. The moment I spotted him boarding the coach I knew I had to have him. The feeling went straight to my crotch. He was dead gorgeous – muscly (I usually go for men with a bit of meat on them – Pedro's an exception, of course, though I suppose he has it where it counts, at least in one direction), swarthy (I hate guys with pale complexions) and with this wicked-looking grin permanently on his face (and they absolutely have to have a sense of humour).

For the first couple of days we were like giving each other the eye – passing in the Sol's lobby, by the pool, at the bar, when I was doing my rounds (as we reps call it). I could tell he was coming on to me. Then one afternoon – we do get some time off in this job, about three-quarters of an hour a week – I managed to squeeze into a spot on the beach just in front of him and his gang. The others didn't notice me at first, but he did, straight away. It was as if he'd been looking out for me. I pretended I hadn't noticed him as I unrolled my towel, making sure my bum was pointing at him as I bent over. I used to think my bum was rather low-slung, but I have this great bikini at the moment which seems to disguise that. Don't ask me how, because there's so little of it. Perhaps it's because, when I'm in it, there's no way to tell exactly where my bum starts and my thighs end.

I settled on my tummy, undid my top and let the boiling, and I mean boiling, sun go to work. However, I soon found that I was a bit itchy, down there, and slipped my hand under my tummy, and down the rest of the way. But if you scratch an itch, well, it sort of makes it worse and you have to keep scratching. Anyway, I'm not sure exactly what Warren could see, but the next thing I know he's kicked a slab of sand on to my hot, sweaty, nearly bare arse, and he's weaving through the crowd heading for the water. I didn't even think before I was up after him. But there were so many people playing by the water's edge that I lost him.

Desperately needing to cool off, I waded in anyway. I normally stick to the pool, because I like to be able to see the bottom, but I didn't mind the murkiness then. Whoever said the Med was crystal clear? I was sort of half floating, letting my boobs support me, when Warren suddenly surfaced about six inches away, that stupid grin all over his face. I immediately reached for his shoulders and hooked my legs around his waist. The first thing I felt was his erection, pushing against the waistband of his trunks.

Somehow, with me still clinging on to him like that, he managed to free his cock, push aside my brief bikini bottoms and enter me. There were some lads on an inflatable banana nearby and a para-sailer floating just above us, but we didn't care about them. You see, I'd never done it in the sea before – I didn't even know it was possible. It's the weirdest sensation. It's sort of wet and dry at the same time – all slippery, then abrasive. I'm not sure I'd recommend it, but I have one up on Kim here. She hasn't done it in the Med yet.

I replace the mike in its slot by my seat, knowing I've gone on for too long again. The thing about giving the spiel (as we reps call it) is that part of my mind always switches off and thinks about other things, like Pedro's cock or doing it in the Med. Plus I'm one of those people who once they get going are impossible to shut up. I reach for my bag and my sunglasses, because I'm now flooded with sunlight. Miguel has already put on his shades, but I still don't know how he can see where he's going. I look over my shoulder, checking on the hunk. He's now sprawled across the two seats, his head resting on a scrunched-up jacket. He's fast asleep – I sent him to sleep. Never mind. I've got a whole week to work on this one. And then there'll be another coachload of potential shags. And then another and another. A whole hot, sweaty summer. Bliss.

The Tennis Lesson

Why today? Why the fuck did she arrange to have a tennis lesson today? She is too fucking busy. Too fucking busy to be told to stretch more. To move her feet more. To keep her wrists straight. To play the ball on the rise, not the fall. To arch her back when she serves. To grunt, if it helps.

Greg, as everyone at the club knows, loves women to grunt. Indeed, having signed up for a block of lessons, having embarked on Greg's infamous brush-up course for intermediates, she has become one of Greg's Grunters. The old farts at the club are always complaining about Greg's Grunters. Well, fuck them, Catherine thinks. As stupid as she feels grunting, as false as it all seems, she is quite happy to grunt if it pisses off the old farts.

God, she is in a bad mood. She has too much to do. Accounts to finish. Kids to pick up from school. Neighbours to deal with. A dinner party to organise. And with tennis on top of everything else, well, that is the last straw.

Stupid cow, she says to herself. For taking on too much, as per usual. Silly stupid cow with a fat arse. She guns the Audi down the side-road which leads to the club, enjoying the ferocious jolts as the car tackles the speed bumps. Catherine always enjoys a little bit of pain – in the bottom region. She likes to punish her bottom for being so big. Except it's also, strangely, highly erogenous. She tries not to think about it too often. The pleasure she gets from the pain. She tries not to dwell on it. But it is hard to punish her bum without, really, feeling a tremendous amount of pleasure. A sudden, shocking tingling all over.

Sitting firmly in the driver's seat, with her back well arched, she realises for the first time that driving over speed bumps at forty mph gives her a not inconsiderable thrill. How come she never noticed that before? She spends her whole fucking life driving here and there.

Arriving at the club, Catherine feels not just rushed off her feet and chronically disorganised and just fucking angry with everything, but she also feels mildly aroused. But, of course, the prospect of spending forty-five minutes with Greg, Greg the fucking Gorilla, has absolutely nothing to do with that. She thought tennis pros were meant to be young and good looking, with superior physiques and beautifully smooth brown skin. That was what she had always encountered on holiday, at some plush Mediterranean resort or other. But Greg is a monster. A saggy, hairy ape of a man. She has no idea how he got the job. Actually, she does. The rumour going round the ladies' changing room is that the old farts had rigged it because they were terrified that if the club hired a half-decent-looking young man all the women, all their sad, frustrated wives, that is, would be queuing up to shag him. A number of female members have said that they intend to shag him anyway, sod the hair. Well, Catherine doesn't intend anything of the sort. She just wants to work on her court craft and get rid of some of the lard that has begun so dramatically to accumulate around the lower half of her body.

Angry, aroused, late, Catherine marches into the ladies' changing room. 'Fuck,' she says, looking at the clock, realising she's already missed five minutes of her lesson. She hates wasting money. And she hates being late. And she can't stop swearing. Her language is appalling. Always has been.

She tips the contents of her sports bag on to the bench and pulls off her clothes. Standing in her underwear, she roots around the mound of sports clothes, searching for her tennis bra and knickers. The bra's there, but not the big fucking knickers. 'Sod,' she says. 'Fucking fuck it.' She searches again and again, glances at the clock. Her top is there and her skirt is there and her bra is there, but not her big white fucking knickers from Wigmore Tennis.

She puts the bra on, her top, her socks, her shoes, and then finally her skirt. She didn't even bring her tracksuit bottoms, and she can hardly play in her work skirt, so there's nothing more she can do. She'll just have to play in her white and blue tennis skirt, from Wigmore Tennis, and her thong from Sainsbury's. It's not as if her tennis skirt is that tiny. But actually she's embarrassed. She's embarrassed to be wearing a thong at forty-three, plus with an arse her size. And the fact that the thong comes from Sainsbury's. She's always popping into expensive lingerie shops and departments but usually ends up resorting to Sainsbury's, because it's so much more convenient than M&S.

However, grabbing her racket and a large bottle of Evian, and walking out of the changing room towards court No. 1 – where Greg likes to conduct his grunting sessions – she thinks why the hell shouldn't she wear a bloody thong, even if it does come from Sainsbury's. Everyone else does. Besides, she has always had this idea that if you have a big arse then you have an even bigger VPL. That a big arse completely accentuates the VPL. So since she discovered the thong, about a decade after everyone else, she has not had to worry about an outsized VPL, making her outsized arse look even more gigantic. Hey, she thinks, walking up to the grunt-master general, thongs were designed for people like me.

Where the hell were they when she was a teenager? When she was out on the prowl – not that she ever really was? Too bloody shy. Too bloody conscious of her big arse. Who's she trying to kid? The lard's not a recent thing. It's always been there, in considerable proportions.

'Hello, Greg,' she says. 'Sorry, sorry, sorry. Late again, I know.'

'Don't worry,' says Greg, a hairy smirk spreading across his face. 'It's your money.'

'Well, let's get on with it, then,' says Catherine. She deposits her Evian on a scruffy chair by the edge of the net and starts swiping the air with her racket as she walks back towards the ape man. 'OK,' she says. 'What are we doing today?'

'Let's warm up with some forehand and backhand strokes, and then I want to crack on with your serve. That still needs a lot of attention.'

'Yeah, right,' says Catherine, walking around the net to face Greg. 'Tell me about it.'

Balls start to be lobbed over the net to her forehand, and she starts to return them with some accuracy if not exactly style.

'Turn sideways,' Greg says. 'Plant your feet wider apart. More of a back swing, please. Keep your eye on the ball.'

Greg begins to make Catherine stretch a little, switching between her forehand and her backhand, and she finds she is quickly short of breath and beginning to sweat and that a thong was not designed for tennis. With each stroke she feels the skimpy gusset pulling tighter against her arse, her anus, her perineum. Like a hot wire. It becomes increasingly painful. 'Yeah,' she sighs.

'Grunt if you want,' says Greg. 'Grunt all you like.'

Swiping and stretching, Catherine starts to grunt. She grunts a low, moaning sort of a grunt that's not much more than a breathy sigh.

'I think we can pick up the balls and move on to that serve,' says Greg.

But Catherine doesn't want to stop. She wants to feel that hot wire cutting into her. She wants to keep moving. So she swings her racket with renewed vigour, grunting and moaning, pretending to hit forehands and backhands, until Greg says, 'It will be quicker if you give me a hand with these balls.'

Feeling ridiculously aroused for the second time that day, Catherine begins picking up balls, finding that if she bends over a little more than is necessary she can get that beautiful burning feeling again. Unaware of being watched by a couple of old farts in the car park, or the fact that hairy Greg has noticed that his 2 p.m. lesson appears not to be wearing any knickers, and unaware that she is still grunting and moaning, Catherine spends much longer than is necessary trying to retrieve a ball that has got stuck in the bottom of the wire fence separating court No. 1 from court No. 2. Bent right over, and swaying backwards and forwards slightly, tensing her buttocks at the same time, she knows that if she were to just carry on for a few moments longer she could probably make herself come – without even touching herself down there, without applying any more pressure on her peculiarly sensitive perineum. But suddenly remembering where she is, she finally grabs the ball and stands and walks over to Greg, wondering whether the squelching between her legs is audible above the squeak of her tennis shoes. She can feel wetness dripping down her thighs.

'OK,' says Greg. 'Let me see you serve.'

'God,' says Catherine, oddly conscious of an extra bulge in Greg's tennis shorts, 'do we have to do that? Can't we do what we did before? I don't think I'm warmed up enough. I want to keep practising my forehand and my backhand.'

'We're running out of time,' says Greg.

'You know,' says Catherine, spotting the two red-faced old farts in the car park staring at her, realising what an eyeful they must have had, and what an eyeful Greg must have had too, 'perhaps there's something else we can do.' She doesn't have to actually touch him, she thinks – his foul, hairy, rock-hard old cock. Just get him to prod her in the right place with his racket, over by the baseline. She'll pretend she's tying her shoelaces. Who cares who's watching? Who cares who's listening. It's her tennis lesson. She's paying for it.

Prêt à Manger

He knows that they all taste the same, but he can still never make up his mind. And not only that. He always has to choose a combination. One is never enough – story of his life. He needs two, minimum. Though sometimes he gets a sandwich and one of those wrap things – the tuna niçoise or hummus and grilled veg. Or he gets a sandwich and a pasta salad. Or a wrap and a sushi tray, but he never finds that combination very fulfilling – it's just not crunchy enough.

Mark doesn't really like sushi. Well, he doesn't mind the California rolls, with the crab sticks and avocado and a good dollop of mayonnaise, except Prêt à Manger sushi trays don't come with anything that resembles a proper California roll. Not that he can ever remember. They come with tuna rolls and salmon rolls and rolls with bits of limp cucumber in them. And individual bits of sushi – he's not sure of the technical term here, but anyway the sausage-shape ones with a finger of raw fish on top and a dab of that green mustard underneath, sometimes held together with a wafer of seaweed and sometimes not. He doesn't mind the salmon ones, again, or the tuna ones, but he's not so keen on the yellowy-white ones, whatever sort of fish that is. It always looks slightly off to him.

Still, however famished he is, and today, this early lunchtime – he can never wait until much past noon for popping out to get his lunch, if he doesn't have a business lunch, that is – he's fucking starving.

Plus it looks like he's got Prêt à Manger all to himself. The squeaky trademark stainless-steel-tiled floor, the shelves, the glass cabinets of warm croissants and pastries, the coffee machines, the soup dispenser, any stool he wants. Any member of staff he wants. If only.

Mark has always associated food with sex – the tastes, the textures, the way both are so filling. He's a big chap with a big appetite. He's always had an idea that thin people are never really into sex. That they are too bloody fussy, because obviously they are fussy about what they eat, what they put into their mouths. If they are fussy about foodstuffs, then, he reckons, they must be fussy about genitalia.

Not him, not in the slightest. He's just a little indecisive when it comes to picking the right combination for lunch from Prêt. He has wondered about giving up Prêt for, say, Starbucks, or Eat, or even the sandwich bit at Boots, but Prêt has better-looking staff. Some of them are really rather young, and some are a little bit grungy also, in his mind, with their ponytails and multiple piercings, but they do all show endless enthusiasm. To be keen, he has often thought, is as important as being unfussy. Keen, unfussy and a tad grungy. Right up his street.

Right, he says to himself – he's always talking to himself – let's get stuck in.

Oh, the other thing Mark spends perhaps a little too long deciding is which sandwich, once he's settled on a particular type, has the most filling. Actually, it's not just the most filling he looks and feels for, but the best proportions of ingredients. For instance, he can't stand the super-club when it has too much chicken and not enough bacon. Or the crayfish and rocket that has too much rocket and not enough crayfish. Or not enough mayo. Or just not enough filling. Or actually smaller slices of bread than normal – that happens, he sees that a lot. So he spends ages picking up sandwiches and feeling their weight, tipping them about in their cartons, studying the proportions of ingredients, the sizes of the triangles of bread. Whether the bread looks absolutely fresh and not in the slightest bit dry.

Mark is not fussy, but he does like things to be right. And he does have a phenomenal appetite. So he needs a number of things that are just right.

But, and here's the crux, he just doesn't think he's anything like so particular, so fussy, and then – and then sex gets in the way. As it always does.

He's by the sandwiches, checking out the turkey club and the all-day breakfast and the big prawn, when a Prêt employee, a young man in jeans and with one of those white Prêt shirts, and with a ponytail, and God knows how many earrings looped around the outside of his ears, and a couple in his nostrils also, comes up with a tray of sandwiches, a tray of more than mozzarella sandwiches – something that has never appealed to Mark – and he smiles at Mark. He nods his head slightly too, setting off the earrings, the multiple tiny hoops all jangling like mad.

If this Prêt had a toilet, Mark would make some remark, would acknowledge the man's interest and suggest that they meet there in, say, a couple of minutes. He might even suggest, or intimate at least, that he could bring along a colleague, a fellow Prêt employee, male or female, if he liked. For a cosy, cramped, outrageously sexy threesome.

No, he wouldn't. Despite Mark feeling the blood rushing to his groin, despite Mark feeling a sudden, an almost uncontrollable urge to take this pierced young man – and for a very brief moment he wonders where else he might be pierced –

into the toilets, with whoever else, in their low-slung jeans and crisp white Prêt shirts, in their Jockeys and Calvin Kleins, in their thongs and skimpies, or perhaps nothing at all (Do some Prêt employees go commando? He's sure they must do.), Mark knows he would never do such a thing.

He's a fantasist. That's what people have been telling him for years. That's what Catherine, his ex-wife and the mother of his children, told him decades ago. 'Mark,' she used to say, 'you live in a dream world. Get real. For fuck's sake.'

Mark used to fantasise about her, of course. He used to fantasise about Catherine in all manner of uncompromising situations, with all sorts of extraordinary people – friends, neighbours, celebrities, politicians. He once had her performing cunnilingus on Norma Major – that's how long ago it was when they were together – with John getting ready to take her from behind, still in his socks, still in those underpants, his small grey stiffy poking out from the saggy fly. He doesn't know for real, of course, but in his fantasies about politicians they mostly always have small penises – except John Redwood and Peter Mandelson. And the blind one, who clearly puts it around a bit.

But it's complete strangers that get him most fired up. Like the idea of slipping into the toilet with this pierced and pony-tailed chap – if only he'd stop arranging the more than mozzarella on the damned shelves – and delving into his hipsters.

Obese, forty-four, balding and bespectacled, Mark knows the chances of this man actually wanting to slip into the toilet with him, for a little light relief before his lunch break, are pretty slight, to say the least.

That's what Catherine used to say too. 'Mark, the thing about you is that you always think people are going to literally fall at your feet. And do whatever you want them to do. You have no idea of the image you project. You have no idea quite how repulsive you are.'

He's not surprised they eventually divorced. It wasn't just because Mark started to discover that he was a tad more bisexual than he'd ever realised, but because she was so damned critical of him all the time. In his favourite fantasy about his ex-wife, he has her having sex with Elton John, while Elton John's boyfriend, that David chap, looks on. Both keep remarking about not just how Catherine's performing – rather lazily for the most part – but about her body, and how it sags in all the wrong places, and bulges in all the wrong places too. 'I just don't know whether I can carry on,' Elton says at one point, pulling out – it's rear entry, of course – to look over his shoulder at his boyfriend, his penis as small and floppy as a raw chipolata.

Why Mark always imagines everyone has a small penis, except Redwood, Mandelson and Blunkett, he doesn't know. Though someone – not Catherine, and not Jacques (the person he had his other significant relationship with) – did once tell him that he was hung like a horse. It was ages ago, when Mark was in much better shape physically. When he was almost fit. He has often wondered since – because nobody else has ever said it – whether his penis has shrunk while the rest of him has expanded. It's not just politicians who he's always thought have small penises but fat people too. As if the fat somehow drains out of their members and back into their bodies, leaving them with a slim, slug-like thing, a raw chipolata, to poke sadly out of their front bottom.

To stop himself thinking about Elton John, Mark looks around the gleaming, empty Prêt, to find the pierced one has disappeared and that the place is not quite so empty any more either. Two or three people have wandered in. Normal office types, who are clearly able to make quick decisions, because one of them has already chosen and is paying for his food. And the other looks as if she's going for the more than mozzarella. She is.

And Mark more than realises he's well and truly missed his

chance, as if there were ever any chance anyway. In the non-existent Prêt à Manger toilet.

Watching the woman pay for her sandwich, in her tight pinstripe skirt and white blouse, he can't help trying to discern what sort of underwear she might be wearing. He loves the back view of a woman, or a man. Of a complete stranger. Loves wondering what someone has on underneath. Or has not got on underneath. There's no VPL. No VTL either, that he can make out. Could she be going commando? In such a respectable, albeit rather tight-fitting skirt? He's transfixed. So much so he finds himself wandering out of Prêt à Manger, following this woman's arse, wondering whether she really is going commando or whether she is wearing a pair of those magic pants that are supposedly invisible yet ultra-supportive.

Out on the now-crowded concourse, losing sight of the woman in the tight skirt, he finds himself completely empty-handed. No more than mozzarella for him. No super-club either. Or turkey club. Or big prawn. Not even any sushi.

Perhaps he'll have to go to Starbucks after all. Or Eat. Or Boots. Who knows what or who he'll find in one of those places. He looks at his watch. It's 12.15. He's already been out of the office for half an hour. He knows he needs to get a move on. But he gets so distracted.

He's not fussy. All right, he is a little indecisive when it comes to choosing his lunch. But he's definitely not fussy when it comes to sex. He'll take whatever is on offer in that department. Except mostly nothing is on offer. It's no surprise he's always been something of a fantasist. I need a holiday, he says to himself. A change of scene. The Mediterranean.

The Salon

She's going to do it. She's definitely going to do it.

Oh yes, she is. All off. Just about. Except maybe for that strip bit in the middle. The landing strip, is it? The runway? That she's heard all about. Who the fuck hasn't? And then she's heading straight for Debenhams. The lingerie department. It's her Valentine treat for Mikey. Well, a very belated one, sure, but so what. She's doing it just for Mikey. And is he in for a surprise. Been urging her to do it for months, for years, and she's always resisted. Mikey's always saying she's just a hairy old dyke, compared with the girls he's seen perform at the Giraffe. 'Why can't you be like them?' he says – the sleaze ball.

She's not sure why she's changed her mind now. Perhaps because Shannon fessed up. Because her best mate Shannon recently told her she's been shorn, more or less, for almost a decade. A decade! Says Bob loves it. And so did Greg before him. Can't stop them licking you clean, she said. 'Plus it makes the old manual a joy – no stray hairs to get caught in your fingers. A totally smooth ride. You can tinkle away all day, if you fancy,' said Shannon, who's the same age. Her very own words. Tinkling away all day, thinks Alicia. Well, she's obviously not getting enough from Bob.

But the truth is Alicia has always been rather proud of her bush. OK, it has become a little straggly of late. But she is twenty-six, same age as shorn Shannon. Still, never too late to change, she thinks. And she can't wait to see Mikey's reaction. Could she perform at the Giraffe? Of course she could. Maybe, she thinks, heading for the salon, once she's been done, and once she's been to Debenhams, she'll head down to the Giraffe and audition. It would beat teaching year three any day.

No, it wouldn't, and no, she won't. Of course she fucking won't. It pisses her off enough that Mikey seems to be in there every other lunchtime. She doesn't want anything to do with some grungy strip pub, full of leery accountants. But she does want a Brazilian.

Shannon said she might as well go to Wendy's in the high street. That's where she gets hers done, always has. So that's where Alicia is headed, Wendy's, South Norwood, for a full-on waxing. Except it's not going to be done by Wendy, if Wendy actually still exists. It's going to be done by someone called Chantelle.

Chantelle is tall and dark, with thick hair and brown eyes. Alicia thinks she is almost the exact opposite to herself, as she's shortish and mousy with bluey-green eyes. She can't stop looking at the girl as she leads her into the waxing room. Inside, the radio is playing Heart FM. Barry White comes on. He's singing 'Playing Your Game, Baby' – his slow, full, fat voice pours through Alicia, and, for the first time today, rather than trepidation she begins to feel a little bit sexy. And determined to enjoy the experience. She can't wait to see Mikey's reaction. She can't wait for Mikey to give her the Valentine shagging of a lifetime tonight – except it's not Valentine's Day. That was weeks and weeks ago. It's just taken Alicia a bit of time to get round to it.

'OK,' says Chantelle. 'Do you want to slip your jeans and knickers off and get on to here.' She pats the massage table, then winks at Alicia.

Suddenly feeling self-conscious, Alicia nevertheless takes off her jeans and knickers – an old pair of plain white briefs from M&S, which she thought was a rather sensible idea as she reckoned she'd probably need a good wash afterwards and didn't want to muck up any of her posher underwear, despite the fact she knows that when she's out of here she's off to Debenhams to buy a whole new lot anyway, including – indeed, especially – a thong called Splendour, which she saw advertised in the *Standard*, for just £15. It's black and has this wicked diamanté detailing at the back.

Alicia climbs on to the table, on to the plastic sheet, and says, because she can't think of anything else to say, 'Ready.'

'Wow,' says Chantelle, 'for someone with your colouring you've got quite a bush.'

'Oh thanks,' says Alicia. 'Well, it's going. Mikey, my fella, he's been urging me to get it done for a while.'

'Yeah?' says Chantelle. 'Seems a pity.'

'Don't say that now,' says Alicia. 'Will it hurt?'

'Depends how much you want off.'

'All of it. Well, most of it, except that little landing strip bit. I did book in for a Brazilian, though I'm not exactly sure what that looks like.'

'Like this,' says Chantelle.

Standing right by Alicia's head, Chantelle suddenly lifts up her white salon dress. She's not wearing any knickers and her pubic area is completely bald and smooth except for a tiny, vertical strip of neatly clipped dark hair, thickening to just a couple of centimetres wide at the top. Teddy Pendergrass is on Heart FM now, singing 'Come Go with Me'. It's 1970s hour and Alicia can't help noticing how dark Chantelle's fanny lips are. She thinks she should turn away but she can't help staring. 'What's it feel like?' she says.

'Like this,' says Chantelle, reaching for Alicia's hand and then placing it against her fanny.

That's not what Alicia meant. She meant: what does it feel like to have it done, to have your bloody pubes pulled out by boiling-hot wax and a length of lint. But Chantelle's fanny does seem remarkably smooth, and hot. It's sort of burning, and Chantelle won't stop pushing Alicia's hand against her. Above the Teddy Pendergrass Alicia is sure she hears Chantelle moan, but she can't look at her face, she can't look her in the eye. She's never been this intimate with a woman before, not since school anyway, not since she was twelve or something, in a changing room, after gym, and before she knows it her hand feels soaking and her fingers seem to be slipping inside Chantelle, and Teddy is moaning about coming and going – or is it Chantelle? – and she just doesn't know where she is and where it's going to lead, whether this is why Shannon really goes to Wendy's, to see Chantelle, and what the fuck Mikey would think if he stumbled in now, which of course he won't because he'll be in the Giraffe with his so-called work colleagues, staring at some eighteen-year-old's bald pussy, his nose up her arse.

Chantelle suddenly lets go of Alicia's hand. 'There's just something I want to do before I whip it off,' she says.

'Please,' says Alicia, 'anything.'

Letting her short white dress fall back into place, Chantelle goes to the corner of the room. Alicia can't see what Chantelle's doing because she has her back to her, though Chantelle soon turns around, holding a large hairbrush.

'I just want to give you a good brushing,' she says. 'You've no idea what pleasure I get from that.'

As Chantelle begins to brush Alicia's pubes, Alicia feels a tingling sensation shoot through her body. With each stroke, as her pubes are slowly, painfully untangled, she knows she's getting more excited, and she parts her legs wider and almost unconsciously lifts her bum off the plastic sheet, trying to press her most intimate, her most sensitive bit of her in the direction of the brush, wanting Chantelle to just move it a little lower, wanting to feel the stiff bristles against her there, barely aware of Minnie Ripperton sweetly singing 'Inside My Love'.

Inside me, Alicia thinks some moments later.

'I just love your pubes,' Chantelle says, now moving the bristles lower, moving the hairbrush in a circular motion.

'Yes,' says Alicia. Yes, she thinks. What the fuck does she want them removed for? For slimy Mikey? And does she really want that black diamanté thong from Debenhams, even if it is only £15? What the hell does she want to look like a sad old stripper for anyway? She's a respectable primary-school teacher. Who happens to have a rather hefty bush.

'If I wasn't in this job,' says Chantelle, having turned the brush around so she's now clasping it by the bristles and letting the handle nudge into Alicia, 'I'd let my pubes grow long and wild. Like I live in the jungle or something. I love pubic hair. I love playing with it, brushing it, getting up close. I thought this would be the best job in the world, but it's beginning to make me sad.'

'Don't,' says Alicia, catching her breath, feeling the warm, wooden handle of the hairbrush probing deep inside her. 'You don't have to remove mine. I think I'm going to leave them just the way they are.'

I am, she thinks. I bloody well am. And I'm going to stick with my plain white briefs from M&S too. Sod the Splendour. Sod the diamanté stripper-look nonsense. Sod slimy bloody Mikey. I'd rather be a hairy old dyke any day. 'Yeah,' she whispers. 'I would. I would.' For now anyway.

Thong Nation: Hozelock

'And another thing I hate,' says Brian, 'is the way you put away empty cereal packets. Why do you do that? Why are they in the damned cupboard? These empty packets of Shreddies and Wheatos and Grape Nuts? So old muggins here can come down to have his breakfast, get out his bowl, his spoon, the milk from the fridge, all by himself, then go over to the cupboard, thinking great, what a choice, thinking I can have anything I want, to find out that actually there is no choice at all, that I can't have anything I want, that there's only a half-empty packet of Weetabix left. Weetabix which is all crumbly too. Weetabix which has gone to seed. I don't know, Sally, I really don't know about this. This gives me a lot of grief.'

Brian's at the kitchen table, sun streaming through the French windows hitting his white shirt, his sunken, pale cheeks, his high forehead.

Brian's at the kitchen table, thinks Sally, being a complete fucking arsehole again. Just like he is most mornings. She's not sure why she still bothers to get up with her husband in the morning. Habit, she supposes. Since she was made redundant she's found it hard to kick all sorts of old routines. Plus she supposes that she'll find another job soon enough – she's not even forty – and will have to get up early again anyway, so why bother getting used to lazy mornings in bed – *sans* Brian.

Besides, it's a lovely day, warm already. Feels like summer. Not even spring. First summer day of the year. This cheers her. She's wearing just her nightie, her shortie nightie, and her fluffy pink-towelling robe, being a redundant slapper (as Brian keeps telling her), and walking over to the French windows she feels the sun on her, penetrating her, warming her right through. Despite Brian, despite Brian's sulky, grumpy fucking presence, she loves the summer. Makes her feel so light and bright, and just a tiny bit frisky. Sex, she thinks, staring at the parched grass, the badly neglected garden, what a desert. Hasn't humped Brian for ages. Doesn't think she ever wants to hump sunken, skinny, balding, boring Brian, with his skinny little limp dick, ever again. She can't wait until he fucks off to work.

'Aren't you going to be late, dear?' she says.

'I'm going to be even later by the time I've had to have breakfast at Starbucks on my way in again,' he says. 'This is not good for my health, Sally. I need a bowl of Shreddies in the morning, not some mouldy muffin from Starbucks.'

'Perhaps you'd like to do the shopping, then?' Sally says. 'For once, perhaps.'

'That's your job, isn't it? I mean, what else do you have to do all day now? What are you going to do today, for instance? While I'm hard at work. Earning money to pay for all this.'

This is Sally's weak spot. Since the redundancy she has felt the need to be occupied, to be busy, to have a sense of purpose, even if it means shopping for Brian's fucking breakfast cereals. 'I don't know,' she says. 'Going to Sainsbury's, I suppose.' She's still by the French windows, letting the sun smack into her, feeling hot under the robe and the shortie nightie. She's not sure whether it's the sun, the brightness, but she feels very irreverent this morning, and oddly sexy. At the back of her mind, but coming slowly to the front, is a need to be very naughty indeed.

'Do the washing as well, I imagine. It's a good day for drying. And maybe I'll even do some gardening, Brian,' she says.

'The grass has all dried up,' says Brian. 'It might not have been a very bright spring, but it's been dry, dry as anything. Haven't had much rain for ages. You should get the old sprinkler out,' he says, cheered.

'That's your department,' she says. 'The lawn's all yours. You know I only deal with the beds and the borders. Men do the lawns, women do the bits and bobs.'

'Sally,' says Brian, 'perhaps it's about time you were a little more adventurous.'

He stands up, finds his suit jacket, creased and out of shape, puts it over his arm. Finds his faded-green Karrimor backpack, which he uses as a briefcase, and, without saying another word, leaves the house, looking a complete mess – Sally thinks. So bloody bald and lanky and dishevelled. Foul.

Yet, she's still feeling hot, and a little bit naughty. Now Brian's gone she feels liberated too. But she also feels a bit guilty about having nothing proper to do, so she walks up to the bathroom, with the washing basket, and starts collecting the dirty laundry. With the weather the way it is, she thinks, she'll be able to do at least a couple of washes today – and some gardening. Smalls first, she decides, and she loads the plastic basket with Brian's disgusting boxer shorts, some of his rancid socks, and some of her bras and knickers and a couple of thongs. She used to wear thongs every day. As all the girls in the office did, but since she stopped going to work she's felt less inclined to wear a thong. She never found them entirely comfortable, and now there is no one to eye her arse, to appreciate the teasing, telltale T of material riding above her slacks, she rarely sees the point in discomforting herself. For Brian? For her lanky, dishevelled, disgusting, smelly old husband? Forget it.

But just looking at the small strips of crumpled material, resting on top of the soft pile of dirty laundry, reminds her of a time when she did want to make the most of herself, of a time when she felt outward-going and, yes, sexy. Holding the laundry basket with one hand, she reaches inside her robe with the other, and, barely having to lift the hem of her shortie nightie, she feels between her legs, feels how dry she is.

She presses her index finger inside herself, for the hell of it, but she's almost as dry inside as she is out. Dry as a bone, dry as a desert – despite feeling a distant tingle of sexual excitement, at least an urge to be naughty, irreverent. She's all dried up. Forgotten about. Useless. Redundant.

She slopes downstairs, bumping the plastic washing basket against the wall, the banisters – disturbing her soiled thongs, which are still on top of the pile, still reminding her that she was once a sexual being. Attractive, up for it. Wet.

Having loaded the washing machine, put it on to Cottons + Linens, 60 degrees, she sheds her robe. The kitchen is stifling, with sun hitting the stainless-steel sink, making it seem like it's white hot. She has to get outside, at least. Doesn't want to be cooped up inside any longer, drying out, going to seed, like old Weetabix, she thinks, crumbling away to dust.

Outside, the still air smells of summer. Of pine sap and cat shit. Sally can't believe how sweltering it is already. It's just gone nine, yet it could be midday, and even her shortie nightie feels too hot and clingy. She would like to take it off, roll around on the dry grass, get some feeling into her body. But the garden is overlooked, at the back anyway, despite the massive plane tree and the weedy acacia, and Sally has never exactly been an exhibitionist. She used to feel confident about her body, sure, happy to show off a bit of thong even, but that was ages ago, back in the days when she used to work. When she was useful, up for it. Capable of becoming wet.

The grass beneath her bare feet feels like stringy dust. Finding herself walking over to the shed, she's amazed it should feel quite so dry and brittle so early in the day, so early in the year, though she supposes Brian had a point when he said it had been a dry spring. Not always bright, but dry. Now it was absolutely scorching, and so, so dry. Everything is dry, Sally thinks. The earth, the grass, the air. Me.

She opens the shed door and is immediately hit by a wave of boiling stale air – powerful enough to make her take a couple of steps back and gasp for something fresher.

'Wow,' she can't help saying. But, having let the fug out and the barely fresher outside air in, she returns to the doorway and, spying the sprinkler, with its Hozelock hose-reel, she makes a dash to the back of the shed, gathers the gear and, with her arms full, reverses out.

Fuck you, Brian, she says to herself as she places the sprinkler in the centre of the garden, and your fucking obsession with fucking Shreddies. Of course I'm fucking adventurous. Crouching, she attempts to unhook the end and uncoil the hose but has to open her legs to get a better balance – fully aware that she has on only her shortie nightie, no knickers, no thong.

Though she is sure no neighbour can possibly see anything, it makes her tingle. It makes her imagine all sorts of wicked things, with weird objects. The end of the hose, the bright-yellow Hozelock bit which has to attach to the tap, Sally decides, has a surprisingly phallic shape.

Before she stands, almost without thinking, she brushes the dusty thing between her legs. Now standing, she has a closer look at it, finding the end no longer dusty but glistening, as if some old water had become dislodged and dripped out. She feels between her legs, wondering whether the thing might have somehow leaked on to her there, upside down.

Just for the hell of it she presses her index finger inside herself again. Though this time she is wet, at least moist, and she realises that she must have leaked on to the Hozelock and not the other way around.

It's still not much past nine in the morning, though the weather says it should be much nearer noon, and, hot and sweaty and oddly damp between her legs, Sally uncoils the hose, carrying the attachment over to the side return where the outside tap is, not being able to resist brushing it between her legs again before having to shove it on to the tap. Though this time she doesn't just brush it between her legs but pushes the tip into her vagina, not caring how dirty the end might be, not caring that the end might have spent the winter gathering dust and dirt in the shed all on its own. A sad, dried-up garden hose thingy.

She suddenly feels very attached to the attachment, working it further inside her, and angling it so the base rubs against her almost-forgotten-about clitoris – standing, legs apart, one hand on the wall, in the side return, definitely out of view from anyone.

However, it's even hotter here, a suntrap this time of the day already, and having felt so dry earlier Sally now feels dripping, all over, and knowing she's not going to have an orgasm – she has to lie down to come, she has to concentrate for hours to come, she couldn't possibly come with the aid of the garden hose, outside – she lets the attachment slide out of her and quickly plugs it on to the tap, as if she hadn't just been doing what she'd been doing with it. She turns the tap on full and, hearing a creaking, groaning sound, sees the sprinkler in the centre of the lawn leap into action, the arc of water beginning to wave in the still, suburban air.

Terribly ashamed of what she had just been doing, ashamed of having been turned on by the Hozelock, wanting to cleanse herself, wanting to cool down more than anything, unadventurous, redundant Sally leaps on to the lawn, and stepping over the sprinkler walks through the arcing spray. It feels so good, she steps back and forth, and back and forth, but each time she crosses through the water, each time the water spurts up on to her, she lingers a little longer and positions herself a little more carefully, so the spray hits her bang between her legs, so the spray hits her hard and soft at the same time right where it counts.

Sally has to lie down to come, Sally has to concentrate for ages and ages to come – normally. But right now, her shortie nightie soaked through, so she might as well not be wearing anything, in the middle of the garden, barely gone nine in the morning, but what a morning, what a scorcher already, Sally comes, sort of standing up, in record time – her spasms in time with the pulsating, groaning, working-overtime, happy-to-be-outside, happy-to-be-being-used, at last, Hozelock garden sprinkler.

Before Lunch

She caught his eye when he was on the thirteenth. She was walking up the fourteenth. With the thirteenth and fourteenth fairways running parallel, but with the play going in opposite directions. Must have cut in, he thought, on the ninth. And then been held up on the fourteenth tee by the four ball ahead – everyone gets held up on the bloody fourteenth. Gorse everywhere. How many balls has he lost off the tee? Hundreds. Possibly thousands. People can spend hours just trying to hit the fairway.

But damned pity, he thought, that he hadn't got to the fourteenth in time to see her drive off. He doesn't often see a bird on the course. Not a young bird wearing such tight trousers and such a skimpy top. Shit, even from a distance Charlie could make out her figure, her behind, her bust. Nothing sexier than a pair of shapely young tits on a golf course. Almost gave him an erection. Without a whiff of Viagra. And that bottom, that gorgeous, curvy young bum, wrapped in some expensive, elaborate underwear, no doubt. Absolutely smashing. 'Good on yer. Whack it for six. Whoooaah.'

Though this is not good for my ticker, Charlie thought as he marched up the fairway, slowing and losing sight of her, and the dog, Dotty, which must have shot off into the undergrowth after some blasted rabbit, the stupid bitch. And Derrick, he thought, where the hell is he? Struggling to control his motorised golf trolley over to the right somewhere, no doubt – that thing leading him all over the place as usual. What a joke. Charlie might have been fucking ancient himself. And completely overweight, over the fucking hill more like, with his cheeks the colour of overripe cherries, and his nose having begun to resemble a rotten strawberry, but he would never be seen with a motorised golf trolley. If he couldn't manhandle his own clubs, well, he'd give the stupid game up and stick to ogling fit young birds. And drinking, of course. And eating. And pumping the old girl once in a blue moon.

Approaching the green, Charlie realised he'd forgotten how hungry he was – having been, mostly, rather pleasantly distracted today. He was always hungry, but by the time he reached the back nine he was always absolutely bloody starving. Especially if it were a Sunday, because on a Sunday he knew exactly what was waiting for him at home, as it had been for years, for decades, for getting on for half a damned century. Every Sunday, bang on one, except he rarely got home before two. He always got stuck in the nineteenth.

'Derrick, you fucking plonker, where the hell are you going? That trolley leading you off into the bushes again?' Bushes, thought Charlie. He wouldn't mind slipping into the bushes with that bird he saw on the fourteenth for a bit of old heave-ho. Ha.

The next few holes were a blur. A disgrace. Charlie lost two balls off the fourteenth, one on the fifteenth and he picked up on the sixteenth. Apart from his incredible hunger, he couldn't stop thinking about that gorgeous creature he had spotted wiggling her wonderful derrière up the fourteenth fairway – knowing that there could well be snarl-up on the short par three seventeenth, where he'd be able to get a much closer look.

The seventeenth, that was his target today. Just to make it to the seventeenth before his damned ticker packed up for good. Though what was he thinking? He was as fit as he was when he was fifty. More than capable of manhandling not just his clubs but a fine piece of skirt too. 'Derrick, does that thing have overdrive? A turbo? Get a fucking move on, will you?'

'Do keep your voice down, Charlie,' said Derrick. 'You're sounding more like a football hooligan every week.'

But Charlie wasn't listening. For up on the seventeenth tee was indeed the bird. Ripe and ready for a good roasting in the bushes. Though who was she with? Her old man?

No, thought Charlie, mounting the wooden steps up to the tee, not her husband, surely. That wouldn't be fair. Though he was positive he just saw this man let his hand brush over her back as she was parking her trolley – in more than just a fatherly way. But the man didn't look much younger than himself. All right, he was wearing a ludicrous pair of bright checked trousers – clearly some sort of fashion item, and certainly not appropriate attire for the old course – but he must have been in his seventies. Surely. Late sixties, anyway. He must have been.

'Good morning,' Charlie wheezed, reaching the top step. He was hopelessly out of breath. He had wanted to bellow, he had wanted to make himself heard. He had wanted to make a bloody impact. After all, he was something at the club. A member of the greens committee, no less. He wasn't just a nonentity. But all he got back from the bird, and the man in the silly trousers, was barely a couple of nods. Bollocks, he thought, turning around to look for Derrick. 'Derrick, hurry up, old chap,' he tried to shout. 'Splendid view up here.'

'Excuse me,' the man in silly trousers said. 'Do you mind?'

'Sorry, sorry, old chap,' Charlie said, as the man approached his ball. After he hit it, a beautiful, high seven iron, which landed just yards from the pin, Charlie said, 'Brilliant shot. Is your daughter as good?'

The man looked at Charlie again, fiercely, before picking up his tee and moving over to his clubs. 'She's my wife, actually. And yes, she is as good. Better. Aren't you, darling?'

The bird smiled at her husband, not at Charlie, and Charlie stepped further back, pretending to look for Derrick. As the bird approached her tee, he heard his stomach rumble, realising his stomach must have just been full of stale air, desperate for its Sunday roast – overcooked to perfection by the old girl. 'Derrick,' he said, as his playing partner climbed the wooden steps to the tee, 'you've made it just in time.'

'Shhhh,' said Derrick, arriving by Charlie's side, 'that woman's about to hit off.'

'Exactly,' said Charlie. 'Christ,' he said, watching her bend down to plant her ball on the tee. 'Did you see that?'

'Shut up,' said Derrick.

'Yes, shut up,' said the man in silly trousers.

'Fantastic,' Charlie said, as the bird's shot landed on the green, also a couple of yards from the pin. It was every bit as good as her husband's. 'Absolutely fantastic.'

'Thank you,' she said, standing back and looking at him this time. She even smiled.

But Charlie wasn't thinking of the shot. He was thinking of the bird's bottom, as she had bent down to plant her tee, and more important, more extraordinarily, the wispy piece of crimson-coloured material that had suddenly risen above the waistband of her gloriously tight slacks. And then there was the even wispier thread of material that slipped down between her buttocks. Right between them. He'd never seen anything like it before on the golf course. Christ. How he'd like to be that strip of material.

'Can you believe it?' said Derrick, as the bird and her husband in the silly trousers headed for the seventeenth green. 'Really. I don't know what this place is coming to. People think they can wear whatever they want. I'm going to have to see the secretary about this.'

'Of course you are, man,' said Charlie. He didn't know whether Derrick was referring to the man's trousers or to his wife's underwear. The trousers, he suspected. Still, despite knowing Derrick was a complete pillock, Charlie hated to disagree with him. In fact, he couldn't afford to, because he owed him rather a lot of money, getting on for a hundred grand, considerably more if interest were taken into account, due to a failed business venture Charlie had got him involved with a number of years ago – making sunroofs for cars that didn't normally come with them. 'Absolutely bloody disgraceful,' said Charlie. 'Haven't seen him here before. Have you? Is he even a member? Looked like a complete clown.'

'I'm not talking about him, you fool,' said Derrick. 'But her. And those knickers, that thong thing she was wearing. On the seventeenth tee, of all places. Flashing it like she were some kind of pole dancer. It's appalling.'

'Oh,' said Charlie. 'That. Them. Yes. Disgraceful. What a . . . what a tart. We certainly don't want people like that here. Christ, no. Completely lowers the tone. Dotty? Where the hell has Dotty got to? You know, Derrick, I think I'm going to have to walk in. God knows where the blasted dog's gone.' And the bird, he thought. Where's the bird now? Sod Dotty. Could he catch up with her before the eighteenth tee? No chance. In the nineteenth, perhaps. He couldn't begin to imagine the chaos that the sight of her thong thing would cause in the smoke room.

But she wasn't in the smoke room. Waiting for her to emerge, hopefully, ever more hopefully, from the ladies' changing room, Charlie sank half a dozen sherbets. He got talking to a right bore, someone from the bunker committee, who bought him another. Then it was suddenly 1.45 and though his hunger had abated somewhat, because he was more than well on the way to getting pissed, his lust for another sight of the bird, and her thong thing, certainly hadn't. What, he wondered, would it feel like to pull it off and slip her a length of his pickled gherkin? Perhaps he wouldn't have to pull it off, just pull it aside. What a fucking fantastic thought.

Driving home without Dotty, Dotty long having been forgotten, he tried to imagine the old girl in a thong. Her large, flabby seventy-year-old buttocks, split in two by a skimpy strip of crimson material. 'Whoooaah.' Being honest with himself, he realised that that was the only piece of arse he was going to get anywhere near today, if not for ever. His philandering days were well and truly over – years before thongs were even invented. But the old girl, good old Dorothy, named after the dog – what does he mean? The dog was named after her – was still good for a good roasting, he thought, laughing to himself, snaking all over the fucking road.

Except when he got home he found Dotty the human, not the dog, not dressed in a skimpy thong thing, of course, ready to massage his pickled gherkin into shape, but bent over the sink, draining broccoli. Still, the musty smell of vegetable water, mingling with the heady aroma of frazzled roast chicken, the half-dozen sherbets he'd tipped back in the nineteenth, the thought of the bird's fit young bottom being tickled rigid by such a stunning piece of equipment, and the homely sight of Dorothy's squashy derrière, bent over the sink, gave Charlie an erection. Or as close to an erection as he'd had unaided since he couldn't remember when – since before the war? Except he wasn't in the war – he was too young – but that never stopped him from pretending he was. For Charlie, reality and fiction were never very removed from each other.

'Dotty,' he said. 'You just stay exactly where you are. Have I got a surprise for you.' Fumbling with the flies of his heavily stained, grey-wool trousers, he somehow eased his gherkin into the open air before he reached his doubled-over wife.

'What the hell are you doing, Charlie?' she said, feeling her husband press up against her. Fearful of spilling the broccoli from the colander into the sink, she didn't turn around.

'I'm starving,' he said.

'Well, lunch is nearly ready. What am I saying? It's been ready for over an hour.'

'For you,' Charlie managed to croak, attempting to lift up his wife's skirt, more than pleasantly surprised to find that her stockings ended just above her knees, and that her pants seemed to be so baggy that he had his hands on her bare bottom in no time.

'Charlie, what the bloody hell's got into you?' she said. But she didn't move. She didn't turn around. She was too amazed to be feeling what certainly felt like her husband's old boy, his pickled gherkin, as he variously loved to call it, sprung to life and prodding her in the backside.

Holding her massive pants to one side, but pretending they were really a skimpy crimson thong thing, pretending indeed that the bottom he was grappling with belonged to the fit young bird, with one hearty push Charlie entered his old girl, at least he slipped his pickled gherkin somewhere between her buttocks, which was when, exactly when, he felt something give way in his chest. A tremendous wrenching.

Slipping to the floor, tumbling into unconsciousness, his suddenly oxygen-starved brain happily, peacefully, contentedly – as if he'd finally seen all that could ever matter – settled on a fantastic thread of material. A strip of crimson that quickly became a blur.

'Thong thing,' the old girl was sure she heard him mumble before he hit the deck.

Part Two
Truly You, Marks & Spencer, £8

CenterParcs

Alicia and Mikey. Shannon and Bob. CenterParcs. In the middle of a forest. Somewhere in the south-east. Maybe.

It was Shannon and Bob's idea. The four of them. For a late-spring break. To cheer themselves up. To get out of the rain. To have a blast. To get toned. To prepare for the summer proper.

They wanted to go somewhere tropical that didn't cost the earth. Or involve flying anywhere. Shannon won't step on a plane and Alicia's not too keen on the idea either – makes her stomach fizz.

So they decide to rent an executive villa – VIP accommodation, as it says – because if they are going to CenterParcs they are going to do it in style. The villa comes with a mini hi-fi, a TV, an outside Jacuzzi (which got them all giggling), a dishwasher (which they have already decided they're not going to use, as they are eating out, every meal, defo), towels, toiletry packs, hairdryer.

The only problem is that one of the bedrooms has a double bed, the other twin beds.

'That's fine,' Shannon says in the car on the way down.

'Alicia and I'll bunk up in the double, and you guys can have the twins.'

'Yeah, right,' says Mikey.

'I'll tell you what,' says Bob. 'Mikey can have both twin beds to himself. A room all on his own, in which he can snore his heart out, and I'll jump in with you two girls.'

'No fucking way,' say Shannon and Alicia together.

'Yeah, no fucking way, mate,' says Mikey.

They are there already, driving through a forest, aiming for the car park. Drop the car off first, it said in the bumf – cars are not allowed in any of the recreation areas, because of the kids, because of the pollution, because this is a true, tropical holiday idyll. Then make your way to the reception.

They park. Grab their luggage, of which they have tons, and stagger to the reception. 'Fucking stupid idea, this,' says Bob. 'Where are the porters? What the hell have you got in here anyway?'

'Are you going to be miserable all weekend?' says Shannon.

'Sex toys,' says Mikey. 'In that massive case. Shannon's. Has to be. A shop full of them.'

'In your dreams,' says Alicia. Alicia knows Mikey fancies Shannon. Everyone fancies Shannon. Even she fancies Shannon, and she's not a dyke. But she's not going to spend the whole weekend watching her fella eye up her best mate. She told Mikey as much, before they left the house that morning. 'No ogling Shannon,' she said. 'Otherwise forget about getting any action with me.'

What Mikey doesn't know, Alicia thinks, is how much she fancies Bob. She fancies the pants off him. Always has done. It's not why Shannon's her best mate. She was mates with Shannon well before Bob came on the scene, but it's one of the reasons she was so keen for them all to go away together. She can't wait to see Bob in his trunks by the pool. Can't wait to squeeze into the Jacuzzi with him. Nevertheless, she doesn't want Mikey getting too close to Shannon. When it comes to her fella, Alicia is dead possessive. She wants everything her way but is not prepared to give anything back.

'Why don't we all go for a swim?' says Alicia, once they've unpacked in their VIP accommodation. Shannon and Bob have got the double bed, of course. Alicia knew Mikey would never have the balls to stand up to them. Still, she's secretly rather pleased. She's so bored with Mikey right now that the last thing she wants is to have to share a tiny double bed with him, VIP accommodation or not. The last thing she wants is to have him pawing her all night, shoving his hands in between her legs, and further round behind.

'Oops,' he keeps saying. 'Oops.' That's not what she says. She says, 'Get away.' At least at home they have a king-size. The largest bed she could find in Dreamland.

'What I want,' says Shannon, 'is to be pampered. Swimming sounds like too much effort to me. I want the spa. What's it called here? What did it say in the brochure?'

'The Tyrolean sauna,' says Mikey. He spotted that in the brochure, all right. And the Turkish hamman, whatever that is. And the Japanese salt room.

Quite frankly he doesn't care, along as Shannon's in there also. He knows she's up for it. That his Alicia is too, really. That sooner or later they are all going to end up in that Jacuzzi, at the very least, naked. Christ, they haven't come to CenterParcs for the cycling.

He's not so sure what he thinks about Bob and his bits and bobs, hanging about all over the place. In fact, he's been trying not to think about that aspect of the orgy. He's always had a slight suspicion that Bob could be gay on the side. That Bob would plug any hole, given half a chance. Him and Shannon, he just knows they are swingers. Have to be.

He can't believe nothing's happened before. Can't believe that this is the first time they've all gone away together.

What Shannon really wants is to be pampered, with Alicia. Somewhere quiet. Somewhere a little dark, with candlelight, perhaps, and the sound of waves, or light rain, or whales, on the sound system. She doesn't fancy Alicia. Alicia's her best mate. However, she would just love to see her body, naked, being gently pummelled by a big, strong, male masseur. See that towel ride up, Alicia begin to moan with pleasure. What is she talking about? Of course she fancies her best mate. She's always fancied her. Alicia knows that. It's just somewhere they don't go. Somewhere they've never gone. It's out of bounds. But whose idea was this short break, anyway?

It was Alicia's, wasn't it? She must have known something was going to happen. Why hadn't they ever all been away before? Because they all knew that it was going to happen, Shannon thinks. She knows that Alicia and Mikey must know about her and Bob's forays into the Norwood swingers' scene. That they have a non-exclusive relationship – as long as they are open and honest about it to each other.

That business in the car, on the way down, with her saying no fucking way to the idea of Bob jumping into bed with her and Alicia, was just her trying to put Alicia at ease. She would love for all of them to be in bed together. Including Mikey, of course.

Bob thinks a swim would be a good idea. He's so bloody excited, if he doesn't do something to calm down, to distract himself from thinking about what's going to be happening later, what's going to be going off in their VIP chalet this evening, at the very latest, he reckons he's going to – he doesn't know what. God, he loves weekends like this. Can't believe they have never thought of it before. They are so naughty. So right up his street.

He thinks a brief walk around the complex, to see what CenterParcs has to offer, before the swim, might be an even better idea. The four of them, out for a innocent stroll before a splash. Like they are the perfect CenterParcs guests. Well behaved. Very respectable. Dead middle class. Ever-so-slightly boring.

With just so much to look forward to.

Besides, he doesn't want to shock any of the kids in the pool with his package. The way it is now, he wouldn't even get it into his new trunks, which are his big surprise for the weekend, his party piece. It would pop up totally over the top. It would look obscene. He'd be arrested.

So they set off, the four of them, Bob and Shannon, Mikey and Alicia, swimming costumes in day bags, libidos all over the place, along leafy CenterParcs tracks, devoid of cars and, well, people, towards the main complex, the village centre, the piazza. Once inside the bubble, the controlled subtropical atmosphere, they find it sweltering. Can't believe how authentic it all feels. They really could be in Bali, or somewhere like Bali, but definitely in south-east Asia, anyway.

They soon find themselves in the Subtropical Swimming Paradise, as it's signposted, and Shannon wants to strip off immediately, saying why bother with the changing rooms. 'If this is meant to be paradise,' she actually says, 'then there wouldn't be changing rooms, would there? We'd just strip off by a palm tree and plunge in naked.'

'Yeah,' says Mikey, 'but it's not. We're in England, somewhere. In a bubble. We can't just do what we want, not in public, anyway.' He laughs. 'We've got to play the game.'

'Where are the changing rooms, then?' says Alicia. 'Let's get on with it. I'm sweating like a pig.'

'Over there,' says Bob, 'if we must.'

Less than ten minutes later, Alicia, Shannon and Mikey are in the pool. At least, they are in one of the pools. The pool they are in is more like a giant Jacuzzi. It is surrounded by foliage, semi-private, and is laced with underwater jets of water. Mikey thinks it's meant to resemble some sort of natural whirlpool.

Shannon doesn't care what it's meant to be. Like Alicia, she's in a new thong bikini, silver – she thought it might not be quite the thing to wear at CenterParcs, then she thought, what the fuck, and packed it anyway. The fact that Alicia's in as skimpy swimwear as herself has both surprised her and excited her. Plus, she thinks, Mikey's looking pretty fit in his shorts and with his hairy chest. Fit, and up for it.

With an underwater jet of water hitting her right on her bum, the most intimate part, which Mikey's not allowed to touch, no way, yet which she is realising is really rather exciting, Alicia's feeling hot and horny. She can't believe that Shannon's got on practically the same bikini. She wonders whether she looks quite as good in hers. Thinks she must look passable, at least – she saw the way Shannon was looking at her – and wonders whether, just maybe, she might be up for a bit of a fumble with her best mate.

It's all going to work out brilliantly, she thinks, adjusting her bottom so the jet of water makes even more of an impact. She doesn't care whether she looks a bit weird, sort of crouching on a ledge in the pool, with Shannon sliding ever closer to her. She can't wait to see Bob, in his trunks, coming out of the changing rooms. Now that's going to really excite her.

Except it doesn't.

'Oh my fucking God,' says Shannon.

'No way,' says Mikey.

'Christ,' says Alicia.

'Hi, guys,' says Bob.

Bob's in a thong. Bob has emerged from the men's changing room, the exit of which is behind a large plastic palm tree, in a pouchy, purple male thong. He actually skips over to the whirlpool.

'You're not getting in here,' says Mikey. 'Not looking like that.'

Shannon's laughing.

Alicia thinks she might start to cry. Everything has suddenly been ruined. There's no way she could fancy a man in a thong. It's a sight, she reckons, which could very easily put her off sex for weeks, for months.

'Hey, guys,' says Bob, beginning to realise that his big surprise might be a big mistake. 'It's only the fashion. Everyone wears these things abroad. In the south of France and places. In Rio.'

'Not in this country, mate,' says Mikey. 'Not at fucking CenterParcs.'

Adios, Pedro, Sort of

Part One

Hi! Can everybody hear me at the back? The front? Underneath? On top? As if.

Shit, am I bored of this already. I even dream about my job. Or rather have nightmares about it. The f-ing spiel. It's stuck inside my head, like it's on a loop. Round and round it goes. Hi! Hi! Hi! Can everybody hear me?

Even today, this morning, when I don't have to go to the airport, so I'm actually having a lie-in, of sorts, it's still in there, going round and round. Like some terrible nightmare.

Stepping outside my room, which is at the back of the hotel and doesn't have a window as such – so, like, I don't know whether it's day or night in there – I'm blinded by the light for a few moments, and the intense heat, before realising it's hot and sunny again, as if it were going to be cold and cloudy. And guess what too? The Med's sparkling merrily away. I can see a few windsurfers going nowhere, some sailing boats going nowhere either, people splashing around by the shore. Bright inflatables. Distant haze. Yawning boredom.

At least I got some sleep last night. Kim, my roommate and

best mate, was out shagging some fella – at his place, or wherever.

She snores like a pig. So when she's not bouncing around on top of some guy – in our room, of all places – she's keeping me awake with her pig-like snorting. I dread to think what her fella make of it. Perhaps she just doesn't sleep when she's with them. She probably doesn't dare.

Shit, it's hot in the sun, so I dip back into the shade by the wall, which separates the hotel grounds from the rubbish and recycling containers – for the whole of Las Gaviotas, that is, and not just the hotel. If the wind's blowing in the wrong direction they really stink the place out. The punters go barmy – you can't even lie by the pool for the whiff. Don't blame them a bit for kicking up a fuss, except, for what they're paying, what do they expect? The f-ing Ritz?

Shit, like I said, am I bored of all this already – barely been here two months. I've got another four to go. Everything's always the same.

Just as I'm approaching the main block, I see a couple of guys – who Kim and me got chatting to the night before last in the foyer – come out of the swing doors and like part so they go either side of me. Both of them brush my arms, and I can't help feeling that if they stepped just a fraction closer they could have stopped me in my tracks, lifted me off my platform flip-flops and carried me off with them, with me facing the wrong way, my feet dangling. I wouldn't have struggled much, really.

They're the best-looking fellas of the current week's crop, which was why me and Kim got chatting to them. But they didn't seem that interested, hence why I've spent the last two nights on my tod, and Kim's been shagging who knows know. Actually, I do know who. She's been with Sean – a rep from TUI. And the guy who's sort of meant to be her boyfriend.

Actually, not really even sort of. He is her boyfriend. And he's started to get monumentally jealous, at least suspicious of her nocturnal behaviour *sans* him – which is not very surprising. And so, after lights out, she has to spend her whole time with him, pretty much, or he's going to dump her, and she decided the other day that actually she doesn't want to be dumped by Sean – she loves him to bits.

I can't believe she came to that conclusion – the guy's an arsehole. Thick as a donkey, as I heard someone say about someone else the other day. Anyway, what it really means is that she's out of action, out of commission, out to fucking lunch if you ask me. Leaving – yes, you've guessed it, poor old me on my tod. OK, that's good news for when we have to share the dungeon, but it's bollocks for me for when I have to go on the pull.

It's hopeless being a bird on your own, even if you are a rep – so I'm discovering. Nobody wants to talk to you. Everybody thinks you are weird. Or desperate. Or both.

Except, of course, it didn't help much being with Kim the other night. We didn't get anywhere with those two guys. Then, looking back, I suppose Kim just wasn't interested – she was thinking about Sean, putting out this non-interested, I'm-otherwise-occupied vibe. So clearly they got the hint and didn't bother trying to go any further.

There's one other thing. Kim's better looking than me. So if no one's interested in her – even though she's the one who's not interested, if you see what I mean – then they're not going to be interested in me. Stands to f-ing reason.

Kim's taller. Not nearly as blonde. In fact, she's a brunette. With blue eyes. And it's not just because she's taller, but she has this incredible body. You should see her stripped down to her thong. Not that she ever wears one – it's hard enough to get her to keep her bikini bottoms on. She's got these long legs that go on for like ever, and a waist, and tits. Big, firm tits that even I wouldn't mind getting a handful of. And she's funny and so much more confident than me, and she gets the best-looking fellas, and, well, to be honest, even arsehole Sean is not bad looking. He's not really that thick either – he speaks Spanish, for fuck's sake. Actually, I'd go as far as to say he's a great guy, with, by all accounts, a very healthy package. I'd go out with him, if I could. Like a shot.

I'm so cross with Kim for having fucking everything. She makes me sick. Almost as sick as the smell in the cafeteria this morning is making me feel. Hotel Gran Sol doesn't have a restaurant. It has a self-service cafeteria. And it stinks. Especially towards the end of breakfast, when none of the tables has been cleared, and a few of the babies have obviously puked up their stale Ready Brek, and half of the grown-ups have either puked up fuck knows what also or just reek of the night before, because fearing they were about to miss a free meal, they'd leaped out of bed and down to the cafeteria in ten seconds flat, without washing, pulling on whatever skanky clothes lay on top of the pile of clothes and beachwear, wedged into the corner of their tiny bedroom. I've seen the state of some of the rooms here. You wouldn't believe it.

And aside from the rank human smells, there's the smell of rancid bacon fat and watery, lukewarm, neon-grey scrambled egg. I kid you not. That stuff glows. And not a very pretty colour.

Do I want breakfast? No. Do I want to punch Kim in the face? Yes.

I hate her. I really do. Why, exactly? Aside from the fact she has fucking everything.

Because I'm bored, bored stiff of Pedro, and she's abandoned me for Sean, just when I need her most. She knew I was planning to dump Pedro. I've been talking about it for long enough. Now, what am I meant to do? Dump Pedro and be totally on my own? It's been bad enough for the last two days – when, I suppose, I've sort of been practising for what life will be like without him. Or her. And it's even more boring and lonely than I could have imagined.

Except I know I can't stand to be with Pedro for another

minute. He disgusts me. That fat, filthy cock of his. OK, I admit, it used to amuse me, even excite me. But not any more. Certainly not since he's been so keen to poke it just about everywhere except up my fanny.

And he's so thick. All right, he can speak Spanish too. Better than Sean, actually. But he doesn't speak English. Barely a fucking word.

Part Two

'Pedro, there's something I've got to tell you,' I say.

Once I've made my mind up about something, I can't wait a moment longer, mostly, and just launch in. So here I am, mid-morning, having burst into the Autos Serra, Alcudia, office – I had to wait for ever for the bus – and walked straight up to Pedro, who was the only person manning the counter. If you ask me, he's the only person who works for Autos Serra. I've never, ever seen anyone else in the office.

I say again, a little louder this time, because, well, I'm not sure Pedro quite understood what I said: his English, as I've implied, is far from perfect, 'Pedro, there's something I've got to tell you.'

I can't believe how brave I'm being. I'm about to dump my boyfriend, when my best mate's just declared undying love for hers. I'm about to become seriously single, not to mention seriously lonely. Why am I doing this?

Because I'm bored. Bored, bored, bored. Pedro is just so boring. We haven't had one proper conversation. We can't even have a laugh together. And then there's this business about him wanting to shove his stubby cock everywhere, except where it's meant to go. Is this a Spanish thing? I wonder. Or just something that older men like doing – because, let's face it, Pedro's no spring chicken. Either way I'd rather shag myself.

'Pedro?' I say. He's still not really paying me any attention.

OK, he's on the phone, but he's always on the phone when I come into the Autos Serra office. 'Pedro.'

What do I have to do to get his attention? What I always have to do, I suppose. I start pouting. And thrusting out my chest – which, even if I have to say so, is looking particularly pert today. I'm wearing one of Kim's T-shirts – her pink one, which says BABE on the front in sequins – and her cut-off denim shorts. Well, why shouldn't I borrow some of Kim's gear? She's abandoned me, hasn't she?

Anyway, Kim might be taller than me, but she's considerably smaller, if you know what I mean, so her stuff is about as tight as you can get on me. And I know Pedro's becoming excited. Who wouldn't be? And maybe it's the exhibitionist in me, but seeing him excited, even though he's still on the phone, makes me want to excite him some more, so I don't just keep thrusting out my chest but start wiggling my arse too, and this sort of makes Kim's tiny shorts sort of dig into me, just where Pedro would like to have his hands, I bet, except his hands are tied, so to speak, so I continue this little show for him, even though I'm meant to be dumping him, and I find I'm becoming a bit aroused myself, actually.

And I think, leaning over the counter to kiss him, on the lips, even though he's still on the fucking phone, that it can't really hurt if I shag him one last time. Wouldn't it be nice if that was the last thing we ever did together, happy memories to go away with and all that? Not that we've ever really done anything else.

So I lift up Kim's top and let him get an eyeful of my tits stuffed into one of Kim's bras, which is a good two sizes too small for me, and I start playing with the button on the waistband of Kim's shorts – undoing it and doing it up again, except each time I undo one more of the other fly buttons, so he gets more and more of an eyeful of my red thong too. It is mine, not Kim's – I do draw the line at borrowing someone else's knickers. Then I've got my shorts off. Just like that.

So I'm in the Autos Serra office, wearing only Kim's pink T-shirt with BABE written on it in gold sequins, a tiny bra and my red thong, well before Spanish lunchtime, on a Tuesday morning – dancing around in front of the boss, who's on the phone, giving me the thumbs up. Anyone could walk in, except I sort of know they won't, because it's not as if Autos Serra is the most popular car-hire firm in Alcudia. By some considerable margin. Plus, it's stuck miles away from anywhere.

Finally, Pedro's conversation comes to an end – I've no idea what he was talking about, of course, though it seemed a little heated. But hey, when doesn't it in Spanish? They all talk so fast, except Sean. His Spanish doesn't sound anything like Pedro's. And I'm suddenly thinking, maybe Pedro's not so thick after all. Maybe he's a pretty smart guy. Talks like one. Plus he has his own business. He looks OK, for a Spaniard. And he has got a humongous cock. What do I want to dump him for, anyway?

The next thing I know he has his hands all over me, at least where Kim's shorts were at their tightest, and he's guiding me around behind the counter to his small office at the back. We've done it in here before, more than once, so we both know where to go and what positions to assume. Which essentially means my arse is sort of perched on his desk, my legs are around his middle – my underwear somehow came off en route – and he does it while he's still standing, with his clothes on, that bulbous cock of his sticking out of his jeans, and into me, and where it's designed to go for once.

Hi, I can't help thinking, I can't help saying to myself even, can everybody hear me at the back?

Pedro, of course, hasn't said a thing yet. Not that I can understand, anyway. But, hey, when does he ever?

On the Rug from Heals

'I'm not going,' says Brian.

'Yes, you are,' says Sally.

'No way.'

'Look, I'm not going to argue about this,' Sally says, 'but you are going. There are only going to be the four of us. You have to come.'

'No,' Brian says. 'Why the hell should I? I'm exhausted. I've been working my arse off all week, unlike you. Why can't I just sit here?'

'Brian, it's three in the afternoon. It's a beautiful sunny day, and you're stuck inside with the curtains pulled.'

'That's to stop the light, the sun, hitting the telly, isn't it?'

'Look at you. All pale and pathetic. Afraid of the light. Afraid of going outside.'

'Sally, I'm not afraid of the light or of going outside. I just want to watch the fucking cricket. Besides, I don't want to go to Lin and Owen's for another bloody barbecue. No way. I definitely don't want to go there, even if it is going to be just the four of us. I never agreed to it.'

'Yes, you did. Ages ago.'

'No, I didn't. Besides, as far as I can recall they only asked us yesterday.'

'That is ages ago, as far as they're concerned. As far as I'm concerned too, for that matter. How much warning do you need?'

It's not just because Sally's been stuck in all week that she's desperate to go out, even if it is to Lin and Owen's for a barbecue, but she thinks Brian should bloody well do something she wants to do for once, and accompany her. She's sick of turning up to these neighbour things on her own. OK, she's sick enough of Brian, all right, but there are times, she thinks, when you have to at least put in appearances as a couple. Plus she can't be bothered to cook for herself and Brian today. And even though Owen's completely crap at barbecuing she'd still rather eat some burned chicken than something she'll have to prepare, because Brian's not going to lift a finger in the kitchen today, that's for sure.

Brian wishes his wife would stop agreeing to things without asking him first. She's always doing this. Besides, why can't she just leave him alone? It is the weekend. He's exhausted. He just wants to slob out in front of the box. Why can't she go to Lin and Owen's if she's so keen, and leave him here?

Because she wants to punish him. That's what it's all about. She wants to punish him because he's earned the right to do nothing all weekend, and she hasn't. And to make herself feel better about having done nothing all week, she wants to drag him along, to make it all seem fine and normal, or something like that – so he thinks.

'You're in the way,' he says. His wife is standing in front of the telly. His view is totally obscured by her fat, denim-clad thighs. Since she was made redundant, Brian has watched his wife balloon. At least the lower half of her. He reckons this is because all she does nowadays is sit around on her arse, eating.

'I'm not moving,' she says, 'until you get up off that sofa.'

Brian's in Lin and Owen's garden, at the far end, by the shed and fountain thing – what a joke. The others are up the other end, on the patio, crowded around the barbecue, engulfed in a cloud of noxious burned chicken fumes. He can't believe he's here. At whatever time it is in the afternoon, when he should be where he was – happily reclined on the sofa, with the room nicely shaded, and beautifully cool, in front of the blasted cricket.

But something extraordinary happened. Rather than storm off in a huff, as he thought she was about to do (despite saying she was not going to budge until he got up off the sofa), his wife, his Sally, to whom he's been married for nine years, for some utterly extraordinary reason started to undo her jeans.

'All right,' she said, 'fuck me, then.'

And she took her jeans off, at whatever time it was in the middle of the afternoon, right there in the sitting room, though with the curtains drawn. And her knickers, off they came too. And she walked up to Brian, grabbed his head and pressed his face into her crotch.

He smelled sweat and fanny, and so taken aback, he in turn grabbed her behind, two large handfuls, and started to lick at her pubic hair, trying to lick the more interesting bits slightly lower down.

Soon they were on the floor, on the rug from Heals – which cost a small fortune – humping away like a couple of teenagers, with the cricket playing to itself in the corner.

It didn't last long. Brian hadn't had sex since, well, he couldn't remember when – and he'd given up masturbating on his fortieth birthday, which was two years ago.

Though despite the brevity of the act, amazingly, Sally did

come. It was the first time she'd had sex, of any sort, since her encounter with the Hozelock attachment one desperately hot spring morning. And recovering her breath, on the hairy, itchy rug – though it cost a fortune, it wasn't exactly the most expensive one in the store, which was why they bought it – she felt remarkably pleased with herself. Not just because she had come, but because of what she had initiated. Because she had done something positive with her anger at her husband, and got something out of it herself. Because she had been adventurous.

She knew then that something quite fundamental had changed, not just within her relationship with Brian but within herself. That far from feeling redundant, she was actually liberated. And getting up, she noticed the rug had a dark, slimy wet patch, about the size of a coaster. It was proof of her adventurousness, her new self. She hoped it wouldn't go away.

Brian's not sure whether he feels duped or what exactly. After they had had sex, Sally said to him, told him in fact, 'Right, let's go,' and, once dressed, he had followed her dutifully out of the front door, the few yards up the road, and into Lin and Owen's – well, what else could he have done? And now here he is – at the bottom of Lin and Owen's garden, not exactly admiring their fountain thingy but trying to avoid the poisonous fumes billowing from the barbecue. Pointedly not joining in. Pointedly standing apart from the group.

But look out, he thinks. It's Lin. She's never been able to leave him alone. She's never been able to leave anyone alone. He and Sally have long speculated about what she really gets up to when Owen's not looking. God, he dreads to think. It's not that she's unattractive, because she's not. She's slim-ish and has very large, rather appealing eyes, and she has sort of blonde hair, obviously dyed, along with small tits and a smallish arse. Overall she's not such a bad package.

Her main problem is that she smells slightly, and not of

perfume. Actually, she always appears a bit unwashed too. A bit dirty. Or rather, as if she's just been doing something a bit dirty and then has not had time, or the inclination, to wash afterwards.

Like Sally and me, thinks Brian with a naughty, semi-ironic chuckle.

'Can I get you anything, Brian? A beer, a glass of wine?'

Of course, Brian couldn't hang around at the bottom of the garden on his own all afternoon. So after a few Stellas he finds himself in the thick of things, on the patio, up by the smouldering barbecue. And he's quite enjoying himself, amazingly, for the second time this afternoon. Sally keeps winking at him. And pouting, ridiculously. He doesn't know how many glasses of Pinot Grigio she's had, but he can tell it's quite a few. Aside from the fact that he doesn't know what's got into her. He feels most confused. But he's not unhappy about it. Even missing the rest of the cricket.

Lin's talking about Marks & Spencer. 'If I wasn't a shareholder,' she's saying, 'I'd have given up going there years ago. It's got so cheap-looking. And you never know where anything is any more. The stores are always such a mess. For ever being rearranged. You can never find anything. No wonder it's in trouble. M&S, what a joke. They should call it S&M for all the pain they inflict.'

'I still buy my underwear there,' says Sally.

'Well, yeah, so do I,' says Lin. 'Who doesn't?'

'I don't,' says Owen, who then takes a long slug of Stella.

'What?' says Lin. 'Where the hell do you get your smelly knickers from?'

'They're Calvin Klein, if you haven't noticed.'

Sally laughs. Brian's amazed. Lin looks puzzled.

While Lin might not be unattractive, in her way, even when she's pulling an odd expression, Owen's hideous, so Sally and Brian have both thought, so everyone's only ever thought.

He's short, with a monstrous stomach, a large head and a peculiarly flared nose. Today he's wearing what he always wears – a faded, blue polo shirt, which is too small for his stomach so the hem hangs over the edge like a sheet over a balcony, khaki shorts, white socks and trainers the size of floats.

The idea that Owen wears Calvin Klein underwear is too much for pissed Sally. She can't stop laughing.

It's too much for Lin too. She's in hysterics. So Brian feels he has to join in, and once he's started he finds the idea pretty hilarious as well.

'It's true,' says Owen. 'I don't know why you all find it so funny. Look, look.' Owen's up off his garden chair, a can of Stella in one hand, the other well-padded paw fishing around with his belt and dipping inside his khaki shorts. 'Look,' he says again, pulling up a band of off-white underpants, the Calvin Klein logo clearly discernible. 'See, see.'

'Christ,' says Lin. 'It's true. Where have I been? What have I been doing?'

'Who wants to see mine?' says Sally. She's off her chair and wobbling about the patio, fumbling with the buttons on her jeans. Wiggling her hips. 'They're from M&S, and I'm particularly proud of them.'

Her voice is slurred, her movements slow, but rather than just pull the waistband of her knickers above her jeans, for everyone to see, rather than even open her fly a little to show a patch of knickers, Sally lowers her jeans to her knees. Over her large arse and down her thick thighs.

Brian doesn't know where to look. Aside from everything else, her knickers are a disgrace. Big, and white, but not quite white or thick, or even large enough to mask his wife's expanse of dark pubic hair. So hairy, in fact, is she, so lush, that Brian wonders whether she's been watering herself down there with MiracleGro. It didn't bother him earlier this afternoon; indeed, he barely noticed – so surprised, so ready to burst was he – but in front of Owen and Lin, out in the open, it more than does now.

There was a time, he seems to remember, when Sally trimmed the stuff. When she even wore G-strings and thongs, when she was employed. But it would be impossible for her to wear such skimpy underwear now. Absurd, at least. He suddenly gets it into his head that his wife is becoming some sort of wild animal.

'What the hell are they?' says Lin. 'Some sort of retro-look bloomers?'

'Bloody comfortable,' says Sally, pulling her jeans back up.

'I quite like them,' says Owen.

Brian realises that Owen is leering at his wife. He has drool, or at least Stella foam, coming out of his mouth.

'These are what you call knickers,' says Lin, standing herself now. And in one crisp, swift movement she's pulled up her dress to above her waist, revealing what Brian can only think of as the sexiest pair of knickers he's ever seen.

They are tiny. A tiny triangle of see-through black material edged in pink, with two slim black bands disappearing around Lin's slim waist. If she has pubic hair, Brian's thinking, she certainly keeps it remarkably well shorn.

He has to glance away for a moment, so aroused is he by the sight, by the contrast between Lin and Sally's underwear, by what's happening to him today. He focuses on Owen and Lin's lawn, realising that it too is well shorn and totally immaculate. And he thinks of his own lawn – unkempt, patchy, wild – wondering whether there is a direct correlation.

Sally's thinking that anyone who wears underwear like that is not getting enough sex; in fact, that they are completely fucking desperate. And she should know, because she used to wear pants like Lin's. Well, not quite like Lin's, not quite so lacy and feminine. But she certainly wore thongs, white ones and red ones and black ones. And she used to regularly have a bikini wax. However, she knows better now. Doesn't she? With a little help from Hozelock – she thinks, laughing to herself, at her own, very secret joke.

Lin turns around, showing Brian and Owen and Sally the rear of her knickers. Except there is no rear. Or rather the rear bit has completely disappeared between Lin's flat but firm buttocks.

Brian can't believe his luck – Lin must be his age, Sally's age. Owen's still leering at Sally. Sally's thinking, how passé. What a tart.

Turning back, Lin says, 'Truly You, M&S, £8.'

'What's she say,' says Owen, 'all yours?'

'You could say that,' says Lin, winking at Brian.

Outpatients

It's hot, and humid, and ponky. 'Yuk,' is all I can say. 'Yuk, yuk, yuk, yuk, yuk.'

I can hardly breathe. From the minute we stepped off the train at Victoria, it's been hell. The traffic, the noise, all these people. It's always hell. But even more hellish when it's hot and sticky and ponky. And it's not even the height of summer. Nowhere near. I hate London. Can't understand why the children live here. Can't understand why anyone lives here.

I'm with the hunt people, the country people. The cunt people, as Charlie has taken to so fondly calling them. 'Dorothy,' he says, watching the news, 'it's those cunt protesters again. They know where to stick it, all right. Good on them.'

So while Charlie's at UCH, seeing yet another heart specialist, I'm whiling away my time on the streets of London. Shopping, supposedly, for something to wear – because my wardrobe's been gobbled up by moths, even my drawers. Except I hate shopping. At my age? With my frame? What am I meant to buy? A tent? A bloody marquee? And it's so crowded. Why is it always so crowded in London? Where do all these people come from? Not the country, not England. That's for sure.

I feel so awkward, so conspicuous, so alien on this wide pavement made narrow with foreigners. I feel like I'm the bloody foreigner, trespassing on someone else's turf. What the hell am I meant to do until lunchtime, when one of my daughters, the grumpy one, has deigned to meet me for a snack? In the café at Fenwicks. Some Italian place. Carlo's, or something. Except knowing Catherine, it's not going to be only a snack. She eats like a horse. The girl has an absolutely massive appetite. Always has had.

'The café,' she said. 'Downstairs, past the knickers.' Café, I'm sure. The place will be hugely expensive.

And did she express any concern for her father on the phone? No. Did she ask what sort of tests he was having done this time? No. Did she wonder how concerned I might be over his ticker problem? No. Did she volunteer to meet me at the hospital once I'd dropped him off? No.

No, no, no, no, no. All she was concerned about was where she was going to stuff her cakehole. And I've got to hang around on bloody Regent Street until it's time to elbow myself over to Fenwicks, where I'll then have to barge my way to the escalators, past the knickers, only to have to wait in some monstrously expensive Italian restaurant pretending to be a café – for Catherine to turn up. She's always late. Fat and late.

As I expected, I arrive first at this Carlo place, in Fenwicks – past the fucking knickers and down the escalator. What sort of name is Fenwicks, anyway? What sort of shop is it? And why is there only one of them, as far as I'm aware?

Hang on a minute. It's bloody obvious. Who'd want another? Stupid name. Stupid shop. With a stupid restaurant, with a foreign name. Carlo's. Honestly. Couldn't they think of anything more original?

I'm not entirely on my own, actually, as the restaurant –

and very expensive-looking it is, too – is already quite full. But Catherine's not here, of course, and I only have the *Telegraph* for company. Charlie's got the *Mail*. The *Mail*'s my paper, but he spotted a story I was reading about animal rights activists, or rather he spotted the photograph of a young Brigitte Bardot that went with it, and he snatched it from me. 'Here,' he said, handing me the *Telegraph*, 'you can have this one.'

The problem I've always found with the *Telegraph* is that there are just too many stories and not enough pictures. It takes too long to read. Though, of course, I can only be thankful of that today. How long have I been here already? Half an hour? Getting on for it. Must be. I'm on page three.

CHINESE WOMEN LINE UP TO TEST FEMALE VIAGRA. That's what it says, though there is no picture, surprise, surprise. Apparently, all these women are besieging a Beijing hospital, which is to start conducting tests into a cream that could enable them to have better sex and orgasms. Supposedly, more than two hundred female volunteers had registered by the end of May.

I can't imagine a cream would help me to have better sex. Crikey. I would need more than that. A new body for starters. Certainly a new bloody vagina. And bosoms.

The age range of these women varies from nineteen to sixty-three, so it says. But I'm sixty-nine. Does that mean I'm too old, anyway? Can't be. Can I? Charlie's supposedly not too old to take the male variety. He pops those little blue pills as if they were Smarties. Whether I'm ready or not. In fact, am I ever ready? Can't have been for years, for decades. I barely feel a thing. I must be completely numb down there. A great, gaping, dusty, numb hole.

Whoops. Here comes Catherine. Don't want her to see what I've been reading. How bloody embarrassing would that be?

*

'How's Dad?' she says eventually, out of breath, wedging herself into the ridiculously fragile-looking seat opposite me. These places always struggle so hard to look modern, to look cool, as they say. Has anyone ever seen a comfortable-looking modern chair? I don't believe they exist. What you want is a good, solid wooden one, preferably with a nice leather seat to it. Like I have at home. Except Catherine would probably struggle to get comfortable on one of those too. She looks bigger than ever – at least, her bottom does. She's always had a particular problem in that department.

'Oh, I didn't know you were concerned,' I say. I'm sure I wasn't as large as Catherine when I was her age. No wonder Mark left her. No wonder she still hasn't found herself a new husband. With a behind like that?

'More tests?' she says.

'Yes. More tests.'

'What are they hoping to find?'

'You know what it's all about. He doesn't want to have the bypass. He's hoping he'll suddenly get better, all by himself. "Not until I'm seventy at least," he keeps saying. He's a coward. Always has been. Look at it this way: he's had two heart attacks already. He's lucky to be alive. A bypass has to be better than, well, dying, doesn't it?'

'But he's seventy quite soon, isn't he?' says Catherine.

'Yes. And who's meant to be organising the party? Me.'

'Oh, God. What does he want to do? I'm absolutely starving, Mum. Should we order?'

'You know what he's like. He wants a big do. With all the family. I think he feels it's his last chance to get everyone together, to heal a few of those old wounds, before he croaks.'

'How do you feel about that?'

'I stopped caring about all that years ago, if I ever did in the first place. You know that. I'm as tough as an old horse.' With a vagina to match, I can't help thinking.

'I do admire you, Mum. So he wants all his children there,

including Zara and Alicia? What about Janet? Is she going to be asked too?'

'Oh yes, all of them. Janet, the bastards. Everyone.'

'Shit, I expect he'll be asking Mark also.'

'Yes. He did mention him. You know what Dad's like. Nothing has ever embarrassed him. He just goes blundering along.'

'He's insane. Who does he think he is?'

'It's probably worse because he thinks he's dying.'

'I wish he would,' Catherine says. 'No, I don't mean that. But it's going to be so bloody awkward for everyone. The prospect is almost putting me off the idea of having lunch. But not quite, Mum. Don't worry. Can we order now? I'm completely starving. Excuse me, excuse me.'

Catherine's trying to hail a waiter. And what a performance she's making of it, in front of all these immaculate, sophisticated-looking, stick-like women. She's never been very subtle, very refined – just like her father. She'd probably have stood up, had she been able to get her bottom out of the chair.

Am I hungry? I suppose so. At least, I bloody ought to be. Haven't eaten a thing since breakfast. But what on earth am I meant to order? Apart from it all being incredibly expensive, the menu's a mile long. And in Italian, or at least a language I don't understand. And I bet Catherine's going to leave me with the bill too – she's always complaining about how broke she is. I can't think why she wanted to come here. Does she think she fits in? Or did she pick it just to make me feel old and frumpy and out of place? One of those cunt people? Besides, she knows I hate Italian food. She can be very cruel.

'Mum,' she says, 'why don't you have the lasagne? Something simple like that?'

'What are you having, dear?'

'I thought I'd start with the spaghetti vongole, and then have the veal.'

'Right. Where's that? Don't think I've seen that.'

'Here,' she says, pointing to and holding up the menu. 'Here, Mum.'

Catherine wants a pudding. I don't know why I'm surprised, but I am. Perhaps it has something to do with the sheer size of her starter, and then her main course. A very large plate of pasta, with shells in it, followed by a very large piece of veal, on the bone. It wasn't an escalope, as she had led me to believe it would be – while I had to make do with the lasagne – but a whole knuckle, with veg and sauté potatoes. She scoffed the lot.

'Do you really need a pudding?' I say, looking at her hard, looking at the lower half of her, which must be more tightly than ever wedged in to the ludicrous modern chair.

'Mum,' she says, 'of course I don't need a pudding. That's not the point. But I want one. And when I want something, I don't see why I shouldn't damn well have it. I've had to put up with enough crap in my life. I'm forty-three. I'm a single parent. I think I've earned the right to have what I bloody well want. Besides, don't you think the waiter's rather gorgeous? Any excuse to get him over here again.'

My daughter has a point. Not that I was thinking about it particularly – no, no, no, of course not – but now she's mentioned it, he is rather handsome, in a rather short, dark, Mediterranean sort of way. Half a century younger than me too, I should think. But he has a nice smile, a nice face. And he's wearing rather tight trousers. You simply can't help noticing.

'See what I mean?' Catherine says.

I nod, not quite believing that Catherine and I are discussing fancying the same man. We've never had such a conversation before. Certainly, we never agreed on her ex-husband Mark. In fact, I always thought he was absolutely disgusting – fat and bald and, as it has turned out, bit of a queer too. I could never see why they got together.

'I've just had an idea,' I say. 'Your father's party. Why don't we all go abroad? It could be a family holiday and party all in one. We could go to somewhere in the Mediterranean. Hire a villa, or stay in a nice hotel.' With lots of waiters on tap, but I don't say that. Nor do I mention what's really on my mind – female Viagra. And getting hold of some. As soon as possible. At least before I croak.

'How are you going to afford it?'

'Well, we'd all chip in. In fact, seeing as it's Charlie's seventieth, everyone else could chip in. Charlie and I could be treated for once. We don't have any money. Never have had, as you know.'

'I've had the most brilliant idea,' I tell Charlie as we leave UCH, the outpatients bit, 'about your party. But I'm not going to tell you. It'll be a surprise. Bugger me, it's still so bloody hot, isn't it? I don't mind the heat in the country or by the sea. Or by the Mediterranean, ha – there's a clue. But in London it's insufferable.'

We walk slowly down the street, heading for the tube. We never take taxis in London – far too expensive. The air is like treacle, but ponky, of course. I can hardly breathe. But I'm feeling remarkably cheerful.

'You're being awfully quiet, Charlie.'

'Nothing to say,' he says.

'How did it really go this time?'

'I told you in there, same as last time,' he says.

'At least you're not getting any worse.'

'I'm not getting any better either.'

'No. Well, think about something else for now. Your birthday, for instance. How about that? Your party, Charlie. I don't want you being miserable all the way home.'

'Great,' he says.

*

Some minutes later, though I don't think we've got any closer to the tube – we're always getting lost in this bloody city – Charlie says, 'They've banned me, you know, from playing golf.'

'Never mind. You've probably played enough golf in your time. You must be a bit bored by it by now. Surely. Hitting all those silly little white balls with a stick. And not very far too, by all accounts.'

'And they've banned me from taking my pills. My little blue ones. My Viagra. What the fuck am I going to do, Dotty?'

'Oh, you don't need to worry about that, old boy.' He's always called me old girl, but I don't often call him old boy, only when I'm feeling affectionate or sorry for him. 'They're making a female version. I'll be able to take it instead.'

'You stupid woman.'

The Giraffe

It's not just sweat he can smell, or fanny. He thinks he can smell shit too. Which is hardly surprising, because he has an arse stuck in his face. It's a firm, shapely, browny-pink, completely hairless arse.

It's wiggling, slowly, and not exactly to the music, which is loud and very slow, and Whitney Houston.

Mikey can't stop focusing on the girl's arsehole, her tight, dark, dry, wrinkled anus. He wants to see it open up. He wants to see it hot and sweaty and covered in K-Y. In fact, he doesn't want to see it so much as fuck it.

He leans closer, so his nose is almost touching it. It is shit he can smell. An earthy, shitty, entirely natural, though obscenely decaying smell. He can feel his cheeks burning. A tingle in his stomach. A swelling in his groin.

The girl turns around and starts pumping the air with her groin. Pumping the space between Mikey's head and her fanny. Way out of time with the dying Whitney Houston singing 'Because I Will Always Love You'.

Her vagina's as bald as her arsehole; no shaving rash, not even a pubic shadow. Her fanny lips are slim and dark – and peculiarly, stunningly neat. Almost perfect. Mikey thinks he can make out a trace of moisture, of fanny juice right there in her top notch crack, as she pumps the air with her groin, as she transfers her weight from one foot to the other. But it is so dark in the Giraffe, it's always so dark in the Giraffe, he can't be sure.

Either way, he wishes she would turn around again, and bend over the way she was doing, and wiggle a bit. He wants the back view, the arsehole, right in his face. And her neat fanny lips hanging underneath. The best view in the world. For one last time. But it is not to be.

The song, which Mikey wasn't paying any attention to at all, ends, and Jocasta jumps off the table, gathers up her underwear and her cash – Mikey splashed out £40 for a double dance, £20 for the dance and £20 tip – waves briefly, the briefest of flickers, then disappears through the crowd and smoke to the girls' changing room.

Mikey hasn't had Jocasta perform for him before. Indeed, he has never seen her before. He has no idea she's really called Jocasta. She told him she was called Julie.

Jocasta knows she could have been a bit more imaginative when she was thinking of her stage name – a bit more slutty – but the night before her audition at the Giraffe she was watching a programme on telly about Julie Andrews and how she's never going to sing again because of some problem with her vocal cords, which got her thinking about how much she used to love *The Sound of Music* as a kid. It was her all-time favourite film. She knew all the songs by heart, but loved 'The Lonely Goatherd' the best, and, of course, 'Edelweiss'. How could anybody not love that? The version where Christopher Plummer and Julie Andrews duet on stage at the Salzburg Music Festival, shortly before they scarper with the kids.

It's 2.30 in the afternoon, but could be midnight in the blacked-out hub of the Giraffe, where the table dancing takes place. Mikey knows he should be pushing off back to work, but the thought of seeing Julie's arsehole close up once more is stopping him from leaving the pub and forcing him up to the bar, where he'll order a bottle of Becks, check how much cash he's got on him, then see if he can book Julie for another dance.

He'll make do with just a single this time. He really will – as long as she gets right down to it double quick and doesn't bother with all that fannying about with her underwear, which some of the girls must think is sexy. You know, he thinks, all that twirling and swirling and the endless rubbing of flimsy thong cloth between their legs. Forget it.

Because he's fucking late already. Aside from the fact that he should be in Bermondsey, checking over a building, he promised Alicia he'd pick up her dry cleaning at Sketchley's this lunchtime. He also promised her he'd have a look in Dixons for a freeview box, as their Sky subscription is up for renewal and Alicia reckons it's not worth paying £30 a month just for a load of boring sport.

Instead he's had his face in fanny and arse. Julie's.

Jocasta's sitting in her underwear – her thong and what she calls her over-knickers, a bra and camisole, all from Knickerbox – in the girls' room, reading Nietzsche. She's actually reading *A Genealogy of Morals*, for her second-year undergraduate modern literature course at UCL. She has a two-hour Nietzsche seminar on Wednesday, which she's particularly excited about.

Unconsciously twiddling with the strap on her camisole with one hand, and the other grasping the Nietzsche, open at the bit about the slave revolt in morality, Jocasta's thinking that the two people who've had the greatest influence on her life so far – except her parents, she supposes – are Nietzsche and Julie Andrews. Nietzsche because until she discovered him she was full of guilt and remarkably timid, and Julie Andrews because, well at least in *The Sound of Music*, she taught her that you could be naive and virginal, and religious, and, of course, dead sexy as well.

Jocasta knows that her interests, her belief in both Nietzsche and Julie Andrews, are slightly contradictory, but it's an approach, a view, that she's sure is at least unique. If she gets that far, she reckons, she might well explore it further via a PhD. *The True Sound of Nietzsche*, she could call it. Or *Nietzsche and Julie Andrews: Making Music*.

'Julie,' says Tina, popping her head around the door of the girls' room, 'some geezer wants you in the snug.' The snug's what they call the blacked-out hub of the Giraffe, where the private table dancing takes place, except it's not very private as up to five private table dances can take place in the space at any one time.

Some of the girls just call it the snatch, not the snug.

'The one you had before,' Tina adds.

'At least he tips properly,' says Jocasta, standing up and putting the Nietzsche on the counter with all the make-up.

And seeing as he does tip properly, Jocasta thinks, walking out of the girls' room on her way to the snug or the snatch – high on *A Genealogy of Morals*, with the words 'High on a hill, the lonely goatherd' ringing in her head – she'll put on a show that he won't forget in a hurry, and which will earn her an even bigger tip than the one she got last time.

As Rod Stewart's 'I Am Sailing' starts up, Jocasta climbs on to the table in front of her punter, who's practically got his tongue hanging out already – which sort of goes with his puce face. If he didn't look quite so desperate, and puce, and wasn't in here paying her to shove her arse in his face, Jocasta reckons she could almost fancy him.

Rod Stewart's not really her sort of music, but then she knows they're never going to play her sort of music in the Giraffe anyway, so she just gets on with putting on the show of her lap-dancing career to date.

To Mikey's amazement Julie doesn't wait until the dying

seconds of the song to remove all her underwear. She's out of it, at least the bottom bits, practically from the word go, then the top's off before he has time to blink.

Her body is incredible. Firm, lithe and extraordinarily hairless. She's got her arse in his face again, already. And this time Mikey's so fired up he can't help but rock forward on his stool, so his nose brushes the oddly cold flesh of her buttocks.

He smells sweat again, and fanny, he's sure – wanting to press his nose, his face into her arse immediately once more. And amazingly, incredibly, extraordinarily, she seems to oblige him, and sort of reverse-pumps her arse into his face, so this time his nose actually does slip between her buttocks and his mouth is practically on her tight, brown, dry, no not dry but suddenly slippery wet, arsehole.

He doesn't just smell shit, he tastes it, as he finds he can't help himself from licking her.

'No, no, no,' he's sure he hears Julie say above Rod's droning, as she jumps away, and spins around, and winks at him. 'Not here, naughty boy.'

The next thing Mikey knows, he's on the street, in broad daylight, having been hauled there by one of the bouncers.

He's outraged. It's not as if he's just any old punter. He's a regular. He's probably the Giraffe's most regular regular. And it's not as if he doesn't tip handsomely either. He's fucking outraged. What's he going to do now at lunchtimes?

He feels a vibration in his trousers, and slowly realises his phone is going. He fishes for his Motorola, locates it, pulls it out, flips it open, without seeing who's calling, puts it to his ear and says, very grossly indeed, 'Yes?'

'It's me,' says Alicia. 'Just checking you got my dry cleaning? And have you been to Dixons yet? Or are you still staring at some bird's arse in the Giraffe?'

Ann Summers

There comes a time in your life – doesn't there? – when you have to start doing exactly what you want. Don't you? I mean, there comes a time in your life when you have to stop thinking about everyone else and start pleasing yourself.

Plus I've been meaning to do this for ages.

All my girlfriends, pretty much everyone I ever come across, says they've dropped in and picked up something or other. Or they've been to one of those parties where dildos are passed around like corn on the cob at a barbecue.

Well, I haven't. I've never just dropped into an Ann Summers store, despite them being everywhere nowadays – you see more of them on the high street than you do Marks & Sparks. I've never been to one of those so-called Ann Summers cocktail dos either. And I'm fifty-eight. So it's not as if I haven't been around for long.

OK, maybe some people might think I am a little too old to be interested in sexy lingerie and, not to be too coy about it, sex toys. Well, I'm not.

I'm not interested in men. I've finally given them up. But I haven't given up on the lingerie – it makes me feel good. It makes me feel young and sexy, even if I no longer want to attract members of the opposite sex, or my own sex for that matter – if you want me to be absolutely clear about it. And I haven't given up on the idea of sex toys. Actually, I haven't even got started yet. Which brings me to where I am right now – marching down Oxford Street, searching for the first Ann Summers I come across. I know there are at least a couple on Oxford Street. I've spotted them from the bus before.

Seeing as this is my first foray into the world of sex toys – what I wouldn't mind knowing was when they stopped being called marital aids and became sex toys – I've decided to make up for lost time. I'm not going to simply shoot in, all embarrassed, and buy the first wimpy little dildo I can get my hands on – I could go to Boots for that – I'm after the Platinum Rampant Rabbit.

I might not have been to Ann Summers before, as I've said, but I've done my research. I read the papers, the magazines. I know what I want – the ultimate bunny, with its six-speed, 6.5-inch main shaft, stuffed with tiny metal balls for super-stimulation, and a clitoral bit, with what looks like rabbit ears and sliding speed control. I've seen pictures, the reports. I've read the test drives.

How did I get by without it? God knows. Because I haven't had a proper man for years, for decades. Do they even exist any more?

My daughters, who are twenty-one and twenty-four, certainly don't think so. Alicia, the elder, is for ever complaining about her bloke, Mikey, saying he might as well be gay for all the interest he shows in her, and Zara says she loses interest in any man within about five minutes.

I used to think their expectations might be a little too high, that girls, that young women today, have been badly conditioned, but over the years, certainly since I ditched Craig, my last husband, I've had a few younger men, and if you ask me they are all show and no substance.

They think they know exactly what they are doing, for ever twiddling with this and that, as if you are some electrical appliance. However, they don't. They are hopelessly lost when it comes to exerting the right pressure when, and more important if you ask me, to acting like a man and just getting on with it, rather than trying to prove how bloody sensitive and understanding they are.

We don't want Einstein. We don't want Freud. We just want multi-orgasms. Which is why I've decided on the Platinum Rampant Rabbit.

Is it that complicated?

Sad to say, but the last proper man I had regular sex with, a man who always showed immense willing, who always got straight down to it, even if he was a little clumsy at times, was Alicia and Zara's dad, Charlie. I was never married to Charlie. I never lived with him, which I suppose might have had something to do with his extraordinary eagerness – his rabbit-like longing to shag me all the fucking time.

But he's another story. A one-off.

Right now, I'm about to take matters into my own hands, so to speak.

Confidence is a funny thing. I woke up with such a sense of purpose. I'd been planning to come into town today for ages. I had earmarked this day as the day I was finally going to go to Ann Summers, weeks ago.

Today was the day, I had long been thinking, when a rabbit would replace the lack of men in my life. I had even been thinking about names for my piece of platinum fun. Bunny was the most obvious, of course, but Bunny seemed too childish, too innocent, too feminine even.

So I had been thinking about Robert, for some strange reason. I don't know any Roberts. I have never slept with a Robert – as far as I can remember. But Robert seemed a manly sort of name. Also, and don't ask me why I thought this, but it struck me as the sort of name that belonged to a man who was well endowed. And my rabbit was obviously going to be very well endowed.

However, I went off Robert when I saw something on TV the other day about Robert Redford. He looked so old and scraggy. If he has a large one, I shouldn't think he manages to get it up much, let alone make it twist and squirm the way my Platinum Rampant Rabbit, with its metal balls embedded all the way down the main shaft, was going to.

Then I thought about calling it Alan. After Alan Hansen. I don't usually watch *Match of the Day*, but Alicia turned me on to him. She said he was the only thing that made football on TV bearable. I got what she meant immediately. Aside from looking gorgeous and hunky, with that dark hair and odd scar on his forehead, he's clearly extremely well endowed. Have you seen the way he sits with his legs so far apart? The poor man has obviously got such a large package he can't even sit down comfortably.

But from what I can tell from the pictures I've seen in magazines, and on the net – my computer skills are quite advanced for a woman of my age – the Platinum Rampant Rabbit is not dark, but bright pink in places. The main shaft is sort of oddly see-through as well.

I just don't think it would remind me of Alan Hansen, however large it feels.

Oddly, but then perhaps not, the person it reminds me of most – and I can only think it's because it's bright pink, and I guess because it will always be ready and eager for action – is Charlie. His face was hideously flushed.

So I'd pretty much settled on calling my Platinum Rampant Rabbit Charlie. When I woke up this morning, with this extraordinary sense of purpose, it was because I was going to reacquaint myself with Charlie – at least, that's how I'd come to think about it over the last few weeks and days.

I know I said I'd given up men, and was now looking forward to doing exactly what I wanted to do, to stop thinking about anyone else, to stop feeling guilty or ashamed or whatever, and to start pleasing myself for once – well, that is all true, but however hard I tried not too I still found I had to associate my Platinum Rampant Rabbit with a human being. I couldn't simply think of it as a machine, any more than I could think of it as an actual rabbit. It had become Charlie, at least Charlie's most important asset.

And now I've found an Ann Summers, on Oxford Street, at lunchtime, in broad daylight – having been so confident and full of purpose, and secretly absolutely fucking desperate to stroll inside and purchase my rather large and crucial artificial organ, which would provide me with not just unlimited sexual pleasure but also the very best available – I'm almost paralysed with shyness and embarrassment.

How the hell can I go in there? I'm a fifty-eight-year-old woman. A twice-married mother of two. I should know better. At least, at my age, I shouldn't have to rely on a battery-operated machine to give me the ultimate orgasm or, as the advertisement material describes, the ride of your life.

Of course, it's no wonder I've never been near an Ann Summers before, or to one of those ludicrous dildo cocktail parties. I've got more pride than that. More sense of my own self-worth.

Look, I might once have run a boutique, and a golf pro shop, but I'm not going to be humiliated by either some teenage shop girl or a piece of jumped-up plastic. And what if I'm spotted?

While I'm more than happy for Oxford Street to be teeming with people, because the more people there are the less likely it is I'll be seen in such a crowd, conversely it's just possible that, given there are so many people out and about, sooner or later I'm going to bump into someone I know.

What if it's Alicia? It couldn't be Zara, because she's safely tucked away in the Med, but it could be Alicia. She could be on an inset day, or throwing a sickie – she's always taking time off. And, plus, I don't want to disparage my daughter, but Ann Summers is exactly the sort of store she'd visit, if she happened to be out shopping. I'm sure she and Mikey have numerous Ann Summer products at home – drawers full, I expect. Though I really don't like to think about it.

And I can't imagine anything more mortifying than my elder daughter catching me paying for a Platinum Rampant Rabbit, even if it's a worldwide bestseller, even if – and I really don't want to think about this, either – she has one herself. A very well-used one too probably – she's her father's daughter all right. As is Zara, the dirty little bunny.

Pull yourself together, woman, I say to myself as I step out of the crowd and into my very first Ann Summers store.

It's quite dark and purple inside, and all I can see are racks and racks of dark-purple knickers and thongs and bras. And lots of young women of Zara and Alicia's age. There is no one remotely my age, and no sign of any sex toys. In fact, it looks a lot like an M&S lingerie department at Christmas time.

Except it's summer. And I'm boiling. And desperately trying to remain cool and confident – to look like the sort of woman who's decided she's reached a certain time in her life when she's made up her mind to stop thinking about other people and to start pleasing herself.

Except, except I can't stop thinking about other people, spotting me in here, among all this dark-purple underwear. I haven't even found the sex toys yet – my Platinum Rampant Rabbit, my ever-ready Charlie. Where is he? Waiting quietly for me on a back shelf? Charlie was never quiet about anything.

I'm not sure whether it's age that has made me so prudish, or the lack of a decent sex life for about two decades, but either way I'm suddenly thinking I'm not quite ready to start pleasing myself, to take matters into my own hands, albeit with the aid of an electric bunny.

It's one thing buying decent, sexy underwear in M&S, or H&M, or at a push Knickerbox; it's quite another to stroll in off the high street and purchase a Platinum Rampant Rabbit from what used to be seen as a sex shop.

Just as I'm about to turn around and run out of here, I'm approached by a sales assistant. The only reason I know she's a sales assistant is because she's wearing a pink badge that says ANN SUMMERS. Otherwise she could very well be a friend of Zara's, or Alicia's, though she's more likely to be a friend of Zara's, with her obviously dyed blonde hair and skimpy T-shirt and extremely low-slung boot-cut jeans. Don't get me wrong. I love the way Zara dresses, the way she looks – I'd give anything to look like that – but she's not exactly subtle – another trait she gets from Charlie, I'd say.

The Zara-lookalike sales assistant says, 'Can I help you with anything?'

Yes, I think. 'No,' I say, 'I'm just looking.'

'The toys are downstairs,' she says, nodding to a staircase at the back of the shop.

'Thank you,' I say. How did she know that that was what I was after? Do I look too old to be buying lingerie from Ann Summers? But not old enough for sex toys?

Now I'm here, I'm thinking, I'm about as embarrassed as I've ever been in my life, so it can't do any more harm if I slip downstairs.

Actually, as I make my way over to the stairs I feel a little better, a touch more confident. I like the lighting in this store, the fact that everyone in here seems to be female. I'd have run it this way.

Now, Janet, I say, descending to the basement, you don't need a man, you need a rabbit.

Oops. There they are. Racks of dildos and vibrators. A whole shelf of them out of their packets and on display, all looking, frankly, ridiculous. There are purple ones, turquoise ones, silver, green and blue ones. A host of pink, flesh-coloured ones.

Some have wrinkles and veins, odd bobbles and bumps, twists and turns. Others are smooth and metallic-looking.

The sizes vary vastly. Some are absolutely enormous, and others so small that they'd get lost. But I don't see anything resembling the Platinum Rampant Rabbit, with its pink bits, see-through stem with embedded silver balls, its protruding rabbit-ear-like clitoral stimulator. I don't see my Charlie.

Zara's friend is suddenly next to me. 'We're out of the Rabbit,' she says. 'Sorry. It's been walking out of the shop. We should be getting some more next week. Would you like to reserve one?'

I'm too old to have to wait any longer, I feel like saying, not believing how disappointed I feel. Instead I say, 'No, don't worry. I'll come back.' I know I won't. I know I'll never get my hands on a Platinum Rampant Rabbit, just as I'll never get my hands on a real man again.

'Have you thought about trying the Robo Cock?' Zara's friend says. 'If you ask me it's a bit more realistic than the bunny. And it doesn't make so much noise.'

'Oh,' I say. 'Which one's that?'

Part Three
Love, Agent Provocateur, £45

Pinot Grigio

Three glasses down and Catherine reckons now's the time to make a move. She wants to get things started before they have dinner. Aside from the fact that the food needs another forty-five minutes, she hates having sex when she feels stuffed.

Leaning across Howard to get to the crisps – she might hate having sex when she's stuffed, but she can't stop eating the crisps; she can't stop eating, full stop – she's careful to brush his knee with her forearm. Sitting back, armed with a handful of crisps, she shuffles her arse, her body, a little closer. It's not easy because her arse is so huge, and the sofa is very saggy, and she's holding a handful of crisps in one hand and a glass of Pinot Grigio in the other. But she thinks she manages some movement in that direction. At least she gets her point across, all right.

Howard leans forward to retrieve his beer from the coffee table – he's stuck with the beer so far, while Catherine's stuck with the wine. She had hoped he'd go for something a little more grown-up, like a Scotch. Or a gin and tonic. Or a glass of red wine at the very least. But he went for the beer. The beer she keeps in the fridge for the gardener, and the man who comes to unblock the gutters, and Jim, who fucks her very occasionally after he's played golf at nearby Dulwich and Sydenham. Mark, her ex-husband, pretty much put her off men who drink beer. It wasn't the quantity he used to drink – Mark was never an especially heavy drinker – but the way he used to burp and fart afterwards and pat his stomach and say, 'Christ, I feel fat.'

Howard smells of soap. And maybe a mild aftershave. Catherine's never been into men who are too fussy about their appearance, or who smell too fancy. She doesn't trust aftershave, what it might be covering up. Mark used aftershave to mask the smell of spunk – which was not his own.

However, Catherine hasn't been this close to a man, a proper, straight (hopefully) male, who's over the age of twenty, since her last tennis lesson with Greg, and despite the fact that he smells faintly of aftershave, and he's drinking a bottle of Sainsbury's French lager, his second, and that he's called Howard, she still fancies him, sort of. More to the point, she still wants to get her leg over before dinner's ready. She's making coq au vin, because she's sick of trendy, insubstantial, Jamie Oliver dishes with silly names and is going back to her calm, fulfilling, honest Delia Smith roots, even if it is supposedly the height of summer and coq au vin has to be much more of a winter dish. Autumnal at the very least.

Plus – and here's a secret – Catherine has always thought Delia Smith is rather sexy, in a very restrained way – that behind the coy smile and dark fringe lurks a devastating sex bomb, up for anything. She hopes she's a little like that too.

They are having mashed potato with the coq au vin. And French beans. And apple crumble for pudding. Too much food for Catherine to even contemplate having sex later tonight. After that lot it would have to be some time tomorrow afternoon, at a push.

So while Howard is still sitting forward, playing with his nearly empty bottle of beer, clearly wanting another though being too polite to ask – God, she thinks, he'll be on his third soon, and she wants him rock hard – she slips her hand behind his back. This, she realises a little too late – but what could she do, she had to get things moving? – is the hand that's still clutching a handful of Sainsbury's Taste the Difference cracked black pepper and rosemary crisps.

Stupid, blundering cow, she says to herself, moving her hand a little higher and over the back of the sofa, and letting go of the crisps and then wiping her hand on the sofa cover, all in a split second pretty much, and hoping the while that Howard hasn't noticed a thing, or at least is too polite to mention it.

'How long have you worked at Winkworth's?' she says. She knows exactly how long – eight years – because not only has she already asked Howard this but she's seen him sitting there for eight fucking years. She didn't fancy him initially. In fact, it's only recently, out of sheer desperation, that she's come to this conclusion.

Chucking the crisps behind the sofa has unnerved her, and she was only trying to get things moving. Christ, she'd got the kids sorted out with sleepovers – no mean feat, as there are three of them – she'd tidied the place up because the cleaner is not due until the day after tomorrow, she'd got the coq au vin in the oven, the crumble ready to go, now all she wants is to get her hands around a real live human cock, before she eats too much to make the mission impossible. She simply can't come when she's feeling full. Her stomach gets in the way. And her head.

'Too long,' says Howard. 'Way too long.' He sits back, squashing Catherine's arm for a brief moment, before he sits almost bolt upright. 'But I like the area. It's a good part of London. You've got a lovely house. As you know, we'd love to market it.'

Basically, Catherine went into Winkworth's and told Howard she was thinking of selling her house. She got him to come round one day last week. It was the hottest day of the year so far, and Catherine made sure she was wearing as little as possible – her slip dress from Jaeger, a bra and nothing else – and she made sure she led Howard up all the stairs, and in the garden she made sure she stood with her back to the sun so her dress would look see-through. What's she meant to do? Sit on her arse, waiting for some nice chap to materialise out of thin air? She's forty fucking three, as she keeps reminding herself, with an arse the size of the back end of a bus – though she's becoming rather proud of it. Especially, thankfully, as it's largely, somehow, cellulite-free. She puts this down to the tennis and to being regularly prodded by Greg.

Anyway, her plan worked, easily. She could see Howard was getting more excited by the minute as she led him around her property. His trousers began to bulge in exactly the right place, and to a not-insignificant proportion. She noticed also that he was not a man of many words – unlike all the other estate agents she had tried it on with before – but those he did utter were decidedly muddled. Besides, he couldn't stop looking at her. When he was leaving she asked him if he'd like to pop round for dinner some time soon.

But it's not working now, Catherine thinks, sitting forward herself and reaching for her wine, the dregs of her third glass. The weather's been awful all week, more suitable to January than early July, though she still decided to wear as little as possible again – her new skirt and floral vest from Monsoon, though sitting forward like this makes her realise that she really should have got the size sixteen skirt, not the size fourteen. Perhaps the size eighteen, but in her experience stuff from Monsoon is always cut on the bias. And she was going to go to town on her underwear. She popped into Agent Provocateur the other day, the one in Knightsbridge, the posh one. Most of the stuff was either too delicate or too ludicrous, though she did spot a range called Love, which, though fancy, being made of Chantilly lace, was, she thought, right up her street. But she couldn't decide on the cream or black thong, and then she thought, Why bother, at £45 for just the thong? She was only trying to shag the estate agent.

Fuck, she thinks, draining the glass, looking at her watch, realising the coq au vin is going to be ready in little more than half an hour, and that she should put the potatoes on for the mash. 'Can I get you another beer? Or something else?' she says, removing her arm from behind him, and standing up, trying to straighten her skirt, at least get it to stop sticking to her thighs. Fuck it, she thinks, I might as well have another glass of wine. Though she can't come if she's had too much wine, either. Food's the real killer, closely followed by alcohol. She reckons she's all right for most of a bottle of Pinot, but any more and nothing's going to be happening very quickly. And she wants something to be happening very quickly indeed.

'Urrgh,' Howard says.

Catherine's in the kitchen bit of the knocked-through room, filling up her glass with Pinot Grigio, thinking, Fuck it, fuck it, fuck it. She hasn't had proper sex for since she can't remember when. Greg, her tennis coach, just gropes and prods her – it's not really sex with him; at the very most it's exercise. Howard's almost her last straw. She's had, or tried to have, all the other half-decent male estate agents in the area – it was a vein she started mining a couple of years ago. To begin with it seemed virtually limitless. Now there's practically no one left.

The kitchen bit of the room smells of coq au vin. But Catherine is not thinking about food for once. Turning back to Howard, she says, 'Look, I've never said or done anything like this before, but I'm not feeling very hungry yet, and I wondered whether we might, you know, just do it before we eat.' She has said this before. More than once. And it has had, she reckons, a seventy per cent success rate. 'I hate having sex when I'm full.'

'Oh,' he says. 'Oh. Urrgh. What, here? Now?'

'If you like,' Catherine says, coming round from the kitchen bit. She walks straight over to Howard, puts one hand on his cheek, the other on his crotch. What else is she meant to do? She's forty fucking three, with a fat fucking arse.

Howard is not hard, or even very big – was she just imagining things the other day? – but he doesn't remove her hand. In fact, he turns his face towards the hand which has been slapped on his cheek. Catherine feels Howard's lips on her hand. She feels him begin to kiss her there. Shocked by the tenderness of the gesture, she takes her hand off his crotch, squashes her skirt up her thighs, as far as she can get it, and straddles him. Removing her other hand from his lips, she leans forward and starts snogging him.

Howard, she quickly discovers, is not a good snogger. His lips are too slack, and his tongue is all over the place, and there is too much spit already. But she can sense he is becoming keener by the second. She thinks she can also feel the bulge in his lap begin to stiffen and grow. Maybe she wasn't imagining things the other day, and he is decently endowed.

She shuffles back a bit on his thighs and puts her hand on his crotch. It's all right. In fact, it's rather exciting. She starts rubbing his penis with the palm of her hand, while she feels Howard try to get his hands inside her skirt and around her arse and inside the back bit of her thong – not the fancy Love one, of course, but one she picked up for nothing from Sainsbury's. His pulling at this strip of material makes the gusset dig into her, in a not unpleasurable way, and she realises she must be wet already.

Within seconds she has got his belt and the fly of his trousers undone and is digging around trying to free his cock from a tangle of white Jockeys.

Out if pops. Light pink and a not-indecent width and length – it's definitely not the largest penis Catherine has ever seen, by any stretch of the imagination, but it's not totally pathetic either, especially as she's desperate – and it's suddenly very stiff indeed. She can't believe her luck. And she certainly can't be bothered with any more appalling snogging or foreplay. 'I'll just get you a condom,' she says, climbing off him and running for the stairs.

She leaves her skirt in the bathroom, and her dirt-cheap Sainsbury's thong, and armed with a Mates returns to the lounge, breathless and wet and just fucking excited about what's about to happen at last. Howard is still on the sofa, his trousers open, his shirt pushed up and his cock thankfully still fully erect. 'Here,' she says, handing him the condom. She can never be bothered to put it on men. It always takes too long if she tries. Men, she finds of course, are much more adept at it. And while Howard might be a crap snogger, he's no slouch when it comes to getting dressed for sex.

She's on top of him again in a second, and he's slipping straight inside her. Since her third kid, since she had Victoria, she knows she's not as tight as she once was. In fact, she reckons her vagina is the size of a Wellington boot. Still, she loves being on top, and at this angle, with him sitting on the sofa, she can immediately feel pressure right where it counts, bang on her bean.

She begins to rock back and forth and Howard tries to push in and out of her, almost trying to lift her off him and lower her back on. She hears him grunt with the effort, but she's feeling so good, doing her rocking thing, she doesn't particularly aid him. She could just rise up and down a bit herself – her feet are still on the floor. Though she continues to rock back and forth, pressing her clitoris against him, knowing, sensing that this way she'll be coming before she knows it.

Except she doesn't come. However hard and fast she goes at it and Howard's still doing his lifting thing, quicker and with more vigour, and she smells the coq au vin, suddenly that's all she can smell and think about, and she begins to think she won't come, and that perhaps she's had one glass of

Pinot Grigio too many. After having gone to all this effort, barring an Agent Provocateur purchase, she's fucking well blown it.

No, she hasn't. She feels the welling in her stomach. The blood pouring into her clitoris. The nerves becoming electric. A swelling deep inside her. Howard's cock pumping. And she screams, urging her orgasm on, and on, wondering as it begins to subside, and before it wells up again, what sort of noise Delia Smith makes when she comes, presuming she still has sex, or at least when she did have sex, back in her coy, dark-fringed heyday. Would it be a scream, or a moan, or perhaps a chant?

Church's

'Can I help you, sir?'

Another lunch hour, without a business lunch. Another hour or so for Mark to kill, wandering around the concourse below 1 Canada Square, Canary Wharf.

It's too hot to go for a stroll outside, far too sweaty. And way too bright. All that concrete and glass and water, and all those people in white fucking shirts.

He's eaten his lunch, two sandwiches from EAT, a prawn one and a smoked cheese and ham one, plus a banana and mango smoothie, and a wedge of carrot cake. He ate that lot shortly past noon, in about five seconds flat, telling his office colleagues he was just having a mid-morning snack. They're used to his habits, the fact that he eats non-stop all morning – endlessly popping down to one sandwich bar or another – then goes out for lunch.

'I'm just looking,' he says to the assistant. He hasn't seen her in here before. And he would have noticed. She's a cracker. Slightly odd face, with a long, thin nose which is set off-kilter, as if she once broke it. But deep, dark eyes, shaded with lots of black eyeliner, and extraordinarily pale skin. Her short hair makes her look boyish, as does her figure. She is long and thin and remarkably flat-chested.

She is wearing a skirt, a short dark-blue skirt. Mark thinks she would be very stylish, in a boyish, dykey way, if she were wearing tights of some description. The fact that she's wearing such a short dark skirt, with bare legs, makes her look a bit tarty, a bit cheap, a little bit dirty. However, he can't blame her for not wearing tights – it is absolutely baking outside. And quite frankly he's always been rather partial to bare flesh – to that dirty look.

He entered Church's not really thinking. He certainly wasn't intending to buy a new pair of shoes or even to try anything on. At the most he was just going to have a nose. But this odd-looking girl/boy, with such long, bare legs, in here on her own and more than ready to serve him has changed his whole outlook. 'Actually,' he says, picking up a shoe, a black half-brogue. He can tell it's a half-brogue because of the stitching.

It seems very well made to him, with welded-leather soles, leather lining and black polished calfskin, and nicely weighted. Jacques got him into shoes. And men, of course. But right now Mark's quite interested in a woman.

'Perhaps I could try a pair of these on?' he says.

'Certainly. What size?'

'I'm normally a nine and a half.'

'And your width?'

'Big,' he says. 'G? I can never remember.'

'I'll get a G, and we can go from there.'

She disappears through a doorway at the back of the store, leaving Mark alone. He looks out on to the concourse. It is surprisingly empty for a lunchtime, then he remembers what sort of a day it is outside and how everyone will be by the fountain, or down by the river, and how he'll most likely have the shop, and the assistant, to himself for the duration. He faces the shoes again, thinking how lucky it is that he's not really buying a pair because he'd never be able to decide exactly which style to go for. But at least he knows he's in the right place. He loves what Church's stands for – quality, craftsmanship, elegance, Englishness. He could go on. But the sales assistant has returned.

'I've brought a nine and a half in both a G and an H. Let's see how we do with these.'

Mark can't quite pin down her accent. The closest he can get to is south London posh. His children sound not dissimilar. She motions for him to take a seat, and, crouching by his feet, Mark can't help staring at her legs, at the expanse of extraordinarily long, white thigh as her skirt rides up. He can see the backs of her thighs too, because she's crouching so low, and at a slight angle to him. Her nose, though, is now meeting him straight on.

And hey, from the underneath, where the backs of her thighs disappear, he can see the gusset of her knickers. It is black, as black as her eyeliner. But pouchy too, as if, he thinks, she has a very handsome pair of labial lips.

He wasn't expecting to see anything of the sort. Though he was instantly intrigued, even excited by the sales assistant, it was because she was so boyish, so sexless in a way, but also rather tarty looking. There was nothing boyish or sexless about what he just saw. He struggles out of his shoes, noticing how wet with sweat his socks are, and clingy. They are stuck to his feet. He hopes they don't smell.

He feels himself flush, with embarrassment and excitement, as she holds out a black, left-foot, Church's custom-grade half-brogue. 'This is the G,' she says. She passes him the shoe and a shoehorn, flashing another pouchy patch of black-knicker gusset. This time Mark wonders whether she did it on purpose, because he hasn't exactly been subtle in where he's been staring.

The shoe doesn't fit. Not even slightly. It seems so small he can barely get his toes in. 'I think I need to try the other pair,' he says.

'Certainly,' she says, taking back the shoe and reaching for the other box, and taking a new shoe out of that and handing it to him, and opening her legs slightly, he's sure, so he doesn't just get a glimpse of the pouchy bit of her gusset, and the outline of her swollen vulva, but a sizeable portion of the front section of her knickers, and the knickers are not just thick black material. Above the black gusset bit is a stretch of very see-through, lace-like material. Behind this material Mark can clearly make out a neat patch of very dark pubic hair.

Shoes normally remind Mark of Jacques and fast, spontaneous gay sex. In fact, for a long time after his first proper experience with Jacques, Mark found the look and smell of smart new shoes an extraordinary turn-on.

They reminded him of the first time they did it, in the toilet of the Vauxhall Tavern. They both, of course, had their shoes on, and Mark remembers staring down at Jacques' shoe-clad feet, either side of his own feet, his crumpled jeans in the middle, and thinking what a very smart pair of shoes. They were highly polished light brown, an elegant, classic shape, possibly Italian, and clearly not just a good fit but very expensive.

When Mark came, because Jacques was ramming him from behind – it was excruciatingly uncomfortable, being one of the first times Mark had had anal sex in a public place – and had his hands around Mark's waist and was manipulating his cock that way, Mark sprayed the toilet seat and the back of the toilet wall and when he opened his eyes he saw that a dollop had landed on Jacques' left shoe, right on the toe, blurring the pristine shininess. Turning the light-brown sheen a dull, misty colour.

The new, wider shoes don't fit either. He can probably get

a bit more of his foot in, but it's still hopeless. He feels so hot and embarrassed and turned on that his face might explode.

'I suppose it's a bit hot for these sorts of shoes,' he says.

'You'd be surprised,' the sales assistant says. 'They do breathe remarkably well.'

'I'm not really sure they're quite what I need right now, thinking about it,' he says. Thinking about what's left of the summer ahead, and the event he's been invited to in Majorca – which he still hasn't quite got his head around but knows he's going to need some sort of summer casual shoes – and just how hot and sweaty and fat his feet are, he says, 'What about loafers? Or more sort of beach shoes, but smart ones. Do you do those?' Ever since Jacques there's been a limit to how casual he's prepared to go with his footwear. Aside from how best to perform anal sex, on the hoof, so to speak – with lots of saliva – Jacques really invested in him the idea that you can tell what sort of a man someone is from the feet up. Jacques used to say that it didn't matter so much what someone's clothes were like as long as they wore decent shoes.

'We have a few styles,' she says, 'but that sort of thing has mostly been in the sale, and we don't have every size.'

Size. The way she said size shot right through him. It wasn't so posh as dirty. Size, he's thinking, as she walks over to the display stand of obviously summer shoes. Mark hadn't noticed this before. Size. The size of her labial lips.

'We've got this sort of thing.' She's back in front of him, holding up a dark-brown suede loafer with very thin, light leather soles. 'Or this.' In the other hand she has a pair of light-brown leather driving shoes, with rubber studs in the soles. The leather has a sort of clearly artificial grain-effect pattern to it.

'Both look fine,' Mark says. 'Can I try both?'

'Nine and half again? These shoes only come in one width.'

'Perhaps you better make that a ten.'

While she's locating the shoes, out of sight, in the

storeroom or wherever it is they keep the shoes at the back of the shop, Mark takes the opportunity to stand up himself and rearrange his penis, which is semi-erect and was caught in the leg of his Calvin Kleins. Once he's freed it, he feels it quickly expand into a full erection. Not bad for a fat, chronically out-of-shape forty-four-year-old, he thinks.

He sits down again and bends forward a little, trying to mask what's going on in his lap. But fuck it, he thinks, sitting a little more upright. She's hardly being very discreet.

Soon she's back in front of him, laden with boxes, which she tries to place carefully on the adjoining seats to Mark's, but one box topples to the floor, and once she's got rid of the others she's back crouching on the floor again, but lower and more indiscreetly than ever, and shit, Mark thinks, she's taken her knickers off. She must have done that in the storeroom. No more pouchy black gusset, just the real, bare thing.

And fucking hell, he thinks, she does have a particularly fine, engorged set of labial lips, like she's had some collagen injections down there – or is it botox? – but she has no pubic hair. What he mistook for pubic hair earlier is in fact a tattoo. Of a snake, or a dragon, or a lizard. He can't quite tell, particularly as she's turned her legs away, her crotch, and is wrestling to get a pair of shoes out of a box, the pair of driving shoes he can see.

He doesn't want a pair of driving shoes. In light-brown leather with silly studs instead of a proper leather sole, however much Jacques might approve of the style. He wants another look at the sales assistant's tattooed crotch. He wants to know exactly what animal or mythical creature has been ingrained on there. He can't believe his luck. Things like this just don't happen to him in his lunch hour. As much as he's always fantasising about various extraordinary scenarios – like shagging the manager from Prêt à Manger in the toilet, having only gone in there to buy a chicken super-club sandwich, a smoothie and perhaps a piece of cheesecake too, or walking into Boots to find everyone in the store is absolutely naked, and getting down to a massive orgy – nothing remotely exciting ever happens. Until now.

'Do you want to try to pop your foot into here?' she says, passing him the driving shoe, waving her bald, tattooed fanny at him again. She's so close he could touch her with his foot.

'Thank you,' he says, taking the shoe. 'Thank you so much.' It's a lizard. He can see that now. A rather chubby lizard, with a red tongue, pointing upwards, so its tail appears to be slipping right inside her, or rather that the lizard has just wriggled out of her. He looks at her wonky face, her black hair and extraordinarily pale skin, still thinking how lucky he is, how things like this just don't normally happen, certainly not in a place like Church's, with its emphasis on quality, craftsmanship, elegance, Englishness.

'What do you think?' she says.

He's not sure what she's referring to, her crotch, which surely must be on offer, perhaps in the storeroom – the gooey bit where the lizard sprang from – or the shoes.

'Do they fit better? Do you want to try the other one?' she says.

Mark can get his foot into this shoe. But it's a tremendous squeeze. 'I don't think these are quite the right size, either,' he says.

'That's such a pity,' she says. 'Because, had they fitted, I'd have taken you into the back and shagged you. But as it is you're like one of the ugly sisters. When I'm on my own I like to play this game. I call it Cinderella. Especially when it's so hot. Heat makes me really horny. I'm not that fussy, either. Just about anyone or anything can satisfy me.'

Mark thinks of the lizard. He wishes he were a lizard.

'But they have to fit. The shoes should really fit first time, like a glove, like a glass slipper. I gave you three goes. Can't say fairer than that.'

Mark can't believe what's happening to him now. A few

moments ago he couldn't believe how lucky he was, that things like this just don't happen to him, not in his lunch hour, not in the shopping mall of 1 Canada Square, Canary Wharf – however much he wishes and fantasises otherwise.

Now it's all evaporated. Reality is coming crashing down. He's been rejected, again.

Did it even happen, he's thinking? Or was all this just a fantasy too? A bad reaction to the heat, to the fact that, as ever, he's so fucking desperate.

'You're like one of the ugly sisters,' she says. 'But, hey, don't look so disappointed. You can touch me if you like. And I won't even make you buy a pair of shoes first. I'll let you do that for free.'

After Gym, After Bill

'After gym,' he said, 'when the kids are on their way to lunch, meet me back in the changing rooms.'

That's what he said, so that's what Alicia is doing. Maybe.

It's the last day of term, at last, and nobody is paying much attention to anything, except Karl. Who's been paying her an awful lot of attention, all week. Karl's a supply teacher, looking after 3B, the class next door to Alicia's, and 3B and 3A do gym together, so Karl knows exactly what Alicia's schedule is, and that once the kids are having their special summer picnic lunch, out on the playground, which has been decorated with bunting and parasols – donated, as usual, by the local pub, the Greyhound – they'll have the changing rooms, in fact the whole of indoors, to themselves.

They're meant to be at the lunch too, of course, looking after their respective classes and joining in the end-of-term fun, but it's always such chaos, and it's one of the few times that the teaching assistants like to get involved, like to assert a bit of control even, and, anyway, Karl and Alicia have other ideas about what really constitutes end-of-term fun. At least, Karl does, and Alicia's not sure.

She fancies Karl, all right. Who wouldn't? He's the most fanciable supply teacher she's ever come across.

The first time she saw him walking down the corridor, on Monday morning, something heaved in her chest and she couldn't believe her luck. Keep walking, she kept saying to herself, until he slipped into Mrs Bevis's class, and she knew he'd be there for the week, because although Mrs Bevis had told administration that she had to have a tooth out on Monday, and that she should easily be feeling fine enough to return to school on Wednesday, she was in fact in Spain, on her summer holiday already, and had absolutely no intention of returning to school until September.

It's not that Alicia doesn't fancy Karl. No, no, no, that's most definitely not the problem – she even fantasised about him when she had a tinkle on Tuesday night, in the bath, before Mikey got home – it's Mikey, of course, her blasted fella. He's the problem.

Although she's been wanting to dump Mikey for months, and is absolutely sure he hasn't been remotely faithful to her over the years, and anyway even if he hasn't been unfaithful, he's at least had his face in some girl's arse at the Giraffe, like every other day, they are scheduled to go on holiday in a couple of weeks – well, it's not exactly a holiday; it's some mad trip to Majorca for her hopeless dad's seventieth birthday – and she can't bear the idea of being abroad, in some crappy hotel, with Mikey for a whole week, if all she wants to do is be with some other bloke.

Because she has a feeling that once, or rather if, she shags Karl, she'll want to keep on doing it.

No, in Alicia's book, there is nothing worse than being with one man, in close, hot confines, all the way abroad, and wanting to be with another.

Actually, she thinks, gathering her things in her classroom, there is something worse. It's being plagued by the idea that you've missed the shag of a lifetime. Why did Karl have to turn up this week, of all weeks, she's thinking as she makes her way to the changing rooms.

She can hear the kids out in the playground getting settled for lunch, the loud voices of various colleagues endeavouring to get them settled, and her heart thumping in her chest. It's not only the prospect of illicit sex with a beautiful young Australian which is making her excited, and wet. She knows the gusset of her thong must be soaked – but thank God she's wearing one, a newish, rather sexy nude one too. Surely she had an inkling something like this might happen today. Well, it had been brewing up to it all week. It feels hot and cold down there, and slippery, all the right telltales.

What's also getting her so excited is the prospect of doing it at work, right under the noses of her boring, fat colleagues. Nothing like this has ever happened at this school before.

But, she thinks, approaching the double doors to the changing rooms, if I go in there, nothing will be the same again. More to the point, how am I going to cope with being in fucking Majorca for Dad's fucking seventieth, and what a ludicrous idea that is, for a whole fucking week, with fucking Mikey?

But, she also thinks, how can I not go in there? She can hear kids still making a hell of a racket outside, knowing that the teaching assistants will be having a hell of a job trying to get them settled, but knowing that she won't be missed yet.

And she's so wet and on fire she knows that nothing is going to take very long.

She walks through the double doors, extra-conscious of the squeak they make opening and closing. The changing rooms seem empty, just smelling of damp and sweat and feet, with hot, bright sunlight blasting through the marbled-glass windows. 'Hello,' she says quietly. 'Karl, you in here?' She walks deeper in, past two aisles of lockers.

'Over here,' comes his reply.

He's behind the last row of lockers, near the sinks, sitting on a bench, looking cool and relaxed, though, Alicia reckons, with an almighty bulge in his shorts. It's pretty obvious even though he's sitting, though as she approaches he stands – his erection hoicking his shorts up, making them appear shorter than normal.

The head teacher doesn't like the staff wearing shorts but makes exceptions for supply teachers, knowing how hard it is to attract decent ones.

'How did you know I'd come?' she says.

'You haven't yet, have you?' he says, laughing, and reaching for her, pulling her towards him. Pulling her in.

Alicia has always liked men who know what they want, who are dead direct, and Karl's Australian accent, and erection, are making him seem very direct indeed. Plus she likes his sense of humour. He's been making her laugh all week, though partly that was because she fancied him so much, and she was nervous and excited and couldn't fucking believe her luck that he seemed to fancy her too. However, it's not as if there is much competition at work. She knows she's the best-looking chick by about ten fucking miles. Chick? All the other females here are either over fifty or over fifty stone.

Karl has his tongue down her throat, working on her wisdom teeth, with one hand on her arse, massaging her light summer skirt from H&M hard into her, round and round and harder and harder, right between her buttocks, massaging her round about there, until she can feel the whale tail of her thong snag and catch and pull in the skirt material, which is in a light floral pattern, and is rather delicate, at least of rather poor quality – really it's a rip-off of a Donna Karan number which every other person seems to be wearing this summer. His other hand is on the small of her back, but working its way very quickly around to the front, and on to her right breast, already. She does like her men direct. And she knows they don't have much time.

And she's got one hand on his back, massaging his T-shirt

into him, and her other hand is on his waist, but moving around to the front of him and moving lower, so it's on his hipbone, and she can feel the tautness of his khaki-coloured shorts material, made taut by his absolutely fucking huge erection, and his tongue probing deeper into her mouth, and his hand on her nipple now and the other moving right between her buttocks from behind, with his fingers pressing almost against her arsehole and then sort of walking down the skirt at the same time, clearly trying to pull her skirt up too for better access, rubbing the material against her, right in between her buttocks, which she is finding is amazingly erotic.

Like that, she's struggling with his belt, the buttons on the fly of his shorts – do shorts normally have button flies? she's thinking – and she can't get anywhere, so she lets her hand drop to the hem of his shorts, to his bare hairy leg, and moves her fingers, her hand up the inside of his shorts, going for his penis that way. She gets hold of his balls first, almost immediately, in fact. Underneath his shorts, Karl is not wearing any underpants.

Something doesn't seem quite right, but Alicia ploughs on anyway, reaching up further until she's grabbed the shaft of his totally rigid cock.

Karl's worked the back of her dress up by now, and he's hooked his hand under the whale tail of her thong and is massaging her bare bottom, letting the odd finger caress deep in the crack of her arse, and the beginning of her completely wet vag, and working her thong off at the same time, but they both keep losing their footing and falling into each other and against the bank of lockers.

Alicia can still hear the kids out in the playground making a hell of a racket, and the sun's still pouring through the marbled windows, making them even hotter.

They stop snogging and Karl says, 'I don't have a condom on me.'

'Shit,' says Alicia. But actually she's pleased. Her discovering that he's not wearing any underpants under his shorts has unnerved her. And since then she's been both trying to work out why it's unnerved her and thinking about Mikey, and their trip to Majorca, and how can she be unfaithful to him just before they are due to leave. 'We can't do it,' she says.

'Sure we can,' Karl says. 'I'll pull out in time.'

'I'm not risking that,' Alicia says, pushing back from him slightly. 'Besides, I barely know you. I don't know where you've been.' Saying this makes her even more unnerved and wary.

'I'm completely clean,' he says.

'All the same,' she says.

'We've got to do something,' he says. 'I can't go out there in this state.'

Neither can Alicia. Despite feeling increasingly confused and a little compromised, she needs some sort of climax. But she wants things to be sorted quickly. She doesn't want to be in the changing rooms with Karl any more, even though she's almost dripping on the floor.

Karl removes his hand from her arse, slides it around to her front, keeping her dress hoicked up, and her thong hoicked down, and goes for her fanny that way, going straight for her clitoris, which he begins to rub a bit too hard, though Alicia quickly gets used to it, and she lets her head fall on to his shoulder, and then she's clinging on, as he works faster and faster. But she knows she's not going to come. She's never come standing up, as far as she can remember.

Shutting her eyes, she feels close to it, but Karl's going too quick, and it's too hot in the changing rooms, and the kids are making too much noise outside, and someone might come in, and Mikey and Majorca are stuck on her brain. So she pretends. She clings to him a little harder, tries to make herself shudder, goes, 'Whoooaaaa.'

A few seconds later, letting his hand drop, Karl says, 'That good?'

'Great,' she says. Reaching to pull her thong up and straightening her skirt, she adds, 'I suppose we'd better be getting back.'

'What about me?' says Karl. 'You can't leave me like this.' Karl doesn't just stand there, looking disappointed, he drops his shorts. Just like that.

Alicia forgets about the fact that he's not wearing any underpants, how weird that is, and concentrates again on how direct he is, how much she likes that in men, directness, and what a beautiful-looking penis he has too. Crouching down in front of Karl, she puts her mouth around the tip of his cock. It tastes of salt, and as she works her tongue over the tip, it tastes saltier, and feels slimy, as more and more pre-come stuff, whatever it's called, leaks out.

By the time she's got a hand to the base of the shaft, and more of his cock in her mouth, he's clutching at the back of her head and moaning, in a clearly audible Australian accent, and Alicia thinks this really is going to take no time at all. But she wishes he wouldn't make so much noise, knowing that anyone overhearing would know exactly who's making the noise, as he's the only Australian anywhere near. Which makes her realise how quiet it must have become outside, that the teaching assistants and the rest of the staff must have got the kids calmed down and settled for lunch. Are they making too much noise in here? Is Karl, with his ridiculous, Australian-sounding moaning, going to give the game away? Mikey doesn't moan. He barely makes any sound at all when he comes in her mouth.

Just as she's thinking this she hears the squeak of the changing rooms double doors, because clearly someone is opening the doors, and coming in, and she pulls her head, her mouth back immediately, pushing Karl away, but still with her hand on the base of his cock, and whether it's because he's ready anyway, or this sudden movement forces it, she doesn't know, but he comes, two, three great spurts. Some lands on her cheek, but as she's standing too, most goes on her top and her skirt.

'Nothing like being caught at it,' Karl says, both of them staring at the corridor end of the last bank of lockers, where whoever it is is surely about to appear, 'by a pupil.'

Sunseeker Portofino 35

I'm up here on the front deck. Stretched out on this super-cool, long white sun mattress. In just my briefest bikini bottoms. With my arms by my sides. One knee in the air. Sunglasses wrapped around my head. My hair tied back. Sun and breeze beating down on my bronzed, toned body. Feeling the motion of the boat as it flies over the waves, the dull vibration of the powerful engines driving it on. Ohhh.

If I opened my eyes everything would be bright and blue. It's the most perfect day. I could be a film star. Or a model. Looking so fucking cool. Reclining up here, one knee in the air, a tingle of wind between my legs, on the front deck of a Sunseeker Portofino 35.

It's Pedro's mate's. Or rather Pedro's mate, Jesus – can you believe that name? – works in a boatyard in Port de Pollenca, and occasionally he gets to test the boats that come in for a service, or a refit, or whatever, and this happens to be one of them – a Sunseeker Portofino 35. It's fucking gorgeous. You should see downstairs. And for today I'm pretending it's all mine. Or at least my fella's. I'm like this rich, beautiful, classy bird – as far as anyone who happens to spot me up here could tell. And it feels great. Like I was always meant to be here. That this is my natural environment. Am I in my element, as we shoot across the sparkling Med, Las Gaviotas just a smudge on the distant shore.

Pedro and Jesus are taking turns driving. You can tell when Pedro's taken over because he likes to do zigzags and things and bang around into what waves there are and the wake of other boats head on. As if he's a kid. Which he is most of the time, even though he's double my age, and is nearly fifty or something. Forty, anyway.

But I can forgive him anything right now. I can even forgive myself for still being with him. Can you believe that? Can you believe I've nearly dumped him, like ten times? Thank fuck I didn't. Because this is absolute bliss. Me on the deck of a Sunseeker, sunning myself, as we head across the bay to some idyllic little cove beyond the headland at Cap Ferrutx, only reachable by super-sleek yacht. Only known about by those in the know. I fucking love it.

To be honest, I'm pleased we're finally here, because it was getting quite rough, and chilly, and wet – spray was going everywhere – and there was nobody about to see me in all my super-sleek, bronzed, wet bikini-bottomed-only, jet-set, film-star, model glory, except the odd dolphin, and who wants to shag a dolphin? Not fucking me. Plus now we've stopped, and it's hot as hell again, I feel a bit burned. Like I need to get out of the sun, or into the drink immediately at the very least. As much as I think my skin's got used to the Majorcan sun, and that I'm as brown as can be, I find I still burn. Amazing, really.

Pedro and Jesus are spending ages fiddling about with the electrically operated anchor. Muttering away in Spanish. Blokes. And gear. The same the world over.

I'm off the front deck and have worked my way around to the back bit – these boats might look fucking amazing from shore, all sleek and shiny and ultra-expensive, but you try walking around one, in open water, on these tiddly walkways like plastic gangplanks. Pretty bloody scary.

Pedro and Jesus are still up in the cockpit bit, still fiddling with the controls, still muttering away in Spanish. I'm like going, Hello! There's a bird on board too, with tits. Or was.

I jump in. Off the teak bathing platform, which Pedro pointed out to me when we first clambered on board. 'This is real class, Zara,' he said. 'Real teak.' The water is not as cool as it looks. But it's brilliantly refreshing nevertheless, and clear. I can see the bottom and it's all sandy ripples. I wouldn't have jumped in had there been weed about, or anything I didn't like the look of – rocks, say. Or stones. Or any sign of any fish. Though now I'm swimming around out here, out of my depth, in this secluded, deserted bay, it's a little freaky. What if Pedro and Jesus suddenly drive off? What if a shark turns up? I know that's not very likely, that you don't get killer sharks in the Med, but what if one got lost, in, say, the Pacific, and swam the wrong way around South America, around the Cape of Good Hope, or through the Panama Canal – thought I was thick, did you? I know my geography, all right. I did geography for A-level, for fuck's sake. Got a B. B for Bimbo. Not.

I start to swim back to the boat, wondering why this bay is quite so deserted. I know it's meant to be only for those in the know, provided they have a fancy yacht, but there is only one other boat, at the far end, almost out of sight. OK, it does look like quite a big boat, even from where I am bobbing around, even from head height in the water – yuk, this sea tastes salty – but where are all the other boats full of super-glamorous people, stretched out naked on fancy white sun mattresses? Where are all the other people to ogle me, in my moment of film-star, jet-set, rich-bitch glory?

I get it.

It's a gay bay.

While I was looking elsewhere for any sign of human life,

Pedro and Jesus have stopped fiddling around with the boat's electrics, or whatever they were really doing in the cockpit, and have made their way to the back, and, wait for it, have taken their trunks off. Really. They are standing butt naked on the real teak bathing platform. They don't have their arms around each other, but they might as well – they are standing that close to each other. Fucking hell.

'Zara,' says Pedro, 'we join you. Is it good?'

Pedro's is fatter, by about a mile, of course. But that's all there is to it – fatness. Like a ball, really, or a fat rugby ball at least. Jesus' is a much better shape. Much longer and thinner, but not too thin. It's a proper penis. Which, frankly, is a little surprising, and sad, because I don't find the rest of him attractive at all. At least, I didn't. The beard put me off immediately. And the long hair, and the fact that he's ancient, and his body is rather scrawny, like he's undernourished. But what a penis. And what a dilemma.

I'm thinking, treading water, they can't be gay. At least, Pedro can't be. Apart from the fact that he shags me whenever he can get his hands on me, I've noticed him checking out just about every woman who walks past. He can't keep his eyes off them. Who knows what he gets up to in that Autos Serra office when I'm not around? So what's he doing naked, standing next to this Jesus bloke? I should have dumped him all those weeks ago. Or is it just a Spanish thing?

'Hey,' says Jesus. 'Is it cold in there?' His English, I have to say, is better than Pedro's.

'No,' I say, 'it's brilliant.' Now I'm back near the boat, with these two butt naked and about to jump in, I don't feel so afraid that a shark might zoom up from nowhere and bite off my legs, or that Pedro and Jesus might drive off and leave me here – in the gay bay.

'Why are you wearing your costume, then,' Jesus says, 'if you are not chilly?'

'Modesty,' I say. 'Know what that means?' I'm not very

good at treading water and talking at the same time. I keep getting mouthfuls of sea water in my gob.

'But there's no one to see you here,' he says. 'This is a very special place. This is not a place for clothes. This is a natural place. This is where you come to get close to nature. And one another. Man and nature together.'

Laughing, Pedro pushes Jesus in before jumping in himself.

I'm thinking man and man together around here. I kick off and swim in a small circle, followed by a larger circle. I can't quite bring myself to swim all the way around the boat. I don't know what might be lurking at the front. Pedro and Jesus are splashing each other and racing off into the distance and back again for more splashing. Like a couple of teenagers.

Fuck this, I think, and I make for the real teak bathing platform and haul myself out on the tiny, wobbly stepladder. It's no joke, and I'm wondering quite how posh and sleek the Sunseeker Portofino 35 really is, and whether having a fancy yacht in the Med is quite such a brilliant thing, especially if all you do with it is drive off to some lonely bay, to watch your boyfriend cavort naked in the water with a man named Jesus. Even if the man named Jesus has a perfectly formed penis. As if, with that name, he'd have a manky one.

I briefly towel myself and without really thinking I make for the outdoor cockpit area. There's a smart, white-padded stool-type seat for the driver and all these controls. I toy with the idea of hauling up the anchor – well, it is meant to be electrically operated – and speeding off. That would serve them right. However, I can't tell how you even turn the boat on. I can't see an ignition switch, or any keys to turn, and knowing I wouldn't do such a thing even if it were clear how, I leave the cockpit and make my way downstairs and inside. When we first came on board I had a brief look in here, but was so keen to be seen out on the deck, especially in the marina at Alcudia, that I didn't linger, and then I got settled up front and then it seemed too rough to go inside, so now finally I'm here.

Wow, is it plush. It takes a few moments longer for my eyes to fully adjust to the dimness. Everything is padded and beige and soft and shiny – at least, what is not soft is shiny. I run my fingers along the woodwork, like glass, and the leather L-shaped sofa, and the top of the dining table, and there is a flat-screen TV on one wall and those tiny Bose speakers everywhere else, and a shelf of cut-glass glasses and decanters, and gold light switches, and a long-haired white carpet – it's almost a shag pile. It probably is shag pile. And this is just the lounge bit.

I take back everything I thought earlier about it perhaps not being so cool to own a boat like this. It's fucking cool, and fucking sexy. Everything's made to measure and fits perfectly. It's brilliantly designed, with these rows of dinky portholes on either side of the room, each with its own curtains. I don't think I've ever been anywhere so luxurious. I could live here for ever.

At the back of the lounge I find a door, a shiny wooden door, with a neat little gold handle, and I turn this handle and open the door, and as I was sort of expecting, but more so, it's a bedroom. Actually, it's more of a bed than a room. It's pretty much all bed, with a white cover on top and masses of pillows, and, not thinking, I dive on the bed and turn over on to my back and stare at the ceiling, the skylight, and the hazy blue sky beyond.

Wow, is it comfortable. Looking around, I notice that the surrounding wall, because it's a curved room, is pretty much all smoked mirror, and I see myself lying here in all this luxury, my little head propped up on the pillows, and my tits blancmanging on my chest, and I'm suddenly conscious that my bikini bottoms are still wet from the sea, and might stain the cover, because they only cost eight euros from C&A in Palma, and are metallic silver, except the metallic stuff, I've already noticed, has a tendency to flake off, so I ease them down my legs and over my feet, and now lying here totally naked, in all this luxury, I can't stop myself from putting my hand between my legs and giving myself a brisk pat on my well-shorn snatch. A well-done-me sort of pat, for getting myself so brilliantly fixed up.

But you know me, one pat leads to another, and pretty soon I'm going at it like my Rampant Rabbit back home, partly because I want to get it over with before I'm caught, and partly because I'm suddenly feeling so turned on I can't help myself.

Because I'm almost on the verge of coming, concentrating like mad, I don't hear anything until the door is pushed open and I'm rudely made aware that I'm not alone, and looking up I see Pedro, a big smirk on his face, and right behind him Jesus – an even bigger smirk on his face.

'We join you?' says Pedro.

'I told you this was a special place,' says Jesus. 'Man and nature together. All of us together.'

'Pedro,' I scream. 'Did you fucking plan this?'

'What's the problem? You don't like the idea?'

I could kill him. But I was so nearly there, and for some reason Jesus' beautiful penis flashes in my mind, so long and neat, perfect, really, like this boat, and I say, 'No, I don't like the idea. But just this once I might make an exception.' What I'm secretly thinking is that maybe I can swap Pedro for Jesus – as long as I can get him to shave off that beard. As long as he's not too fucking gay. When we get back to shore.

Grand Canal

Got to please them some time, Charlie used to think. Bloody women. Got to take them somewhere romantic. Somewhere special. Somewhere fucking expensive. Especially if they are ever to forgive you.

So Charlie decided to take Dorothy to Venice after she found out about Janet, and Alicia and Zara. It was 1988. 'Look, old girl,' he'd said, 'how about a long weekend in Venice? As far as I know there are no golf courses anywhere near. Ha. Just one canal after another. And all that art history stuff. More than enough to keep you happy, I should bloody well hope.'

He decided that if they were going to Venice they might as well go in style, so he booked them into the Gritti Palace. He couldn't afford it, of course, so he borrowed the money, two grand, from Derrick. He told Derrick, who had already invested a considerable sum in Charlie's business – this was when Charlie was manufacturing sunroofs for cars, before many cars came with factory-made sunroofs – that without the money the business could go bust and they'd lose everything. 'What's more,' he told Derrick, 'this Thatcher chap

2230

BOOKS ETC
WHITLEYS OF BAYSWATER
LONDON

PLEASE KEEP THIS RECEIPT

DELTA
4462 7923 5069 4761
0306

SALE £24.96

PLEASE DEBIT ACCOUNT
WITH TOTAL AMOUNT SHOWN

SIGNATURE

M7270
T06223272 R5568
DATE 29/09/[illegible] 5 12:34

seems to have got the right idea. Not standing for any nonsense from the unions, or those fucking miners, or the Argies, let's not forget that. Before we know it the country will be booming. Believe me. Things are definitely on the way up. And we don't want to miss out, do we? Sunshine or not.'

'I know we're in Italy,' said Dorothy on the first day, while they were having dinner in the hotel's fantastically expensive restaurant overlooking the Grand Canal – candles in the breeze, fluttering awnings, the creak and slap of passing gondoliers, that sort of thing – 'but I do wish everything wasn't so Italian. The waiters are looking at me in a funny way.'

'You'd be so lucky,' Charlie said.

'And the food,' she said. 'I'm sure it's very good, darling, and thank you for bringing me here, but it's all pasta and polenta. I can't stand this polenta stuff.' Having finished her liver, she pushed the mound of polenta and onions on her plate to one side. It stank, worse than the Venetian backstreets they found themselves wandering around in that afternoon. They were lost for hours, with the sun beating down and the reek getting worse and worse.

'Think of it as porridge, old girl,' Charlie said.

Dorothy used to hate being called old girl. And she used to hate the way he called her old girl. His ludicrous accent. Because Charlie wasn't posh originally – his father was an accountant. He just pretended to be. Had done so for years, really ever since they were married, at least since he joined the golf club. And the more he pretended, the more Dorothy used to think Charlie actually believed it himself. Charlie was much more of a spiv than a nob. He was so full of shit it wasn't true. Still, he was never stuffy – unlike just about every other male she knew – and he made her laugh. And she supposed she loved him, even though he had betrayed her, with silly little Janet, of all people.

Janet ran the pro shop at the club. She was, effectively, a

shop girl. And not only had he betrayed her – for years – but he'd actually had two children with her, two daughters, on top of the two daughters he already had with her, his wife. All under Dorothy's nose. She hadn't known a thing. God, she felt stupid when she found out. And how.

But Dorothy was made of stern stuff. She knew she could weather the revelations. Bloody hell, her father had done much the same, and her mother had stuck with him. She also knew that Charlie would never leave her, not for a silly shop girl. After all, she had provided him with not only large sums of cash, years ago, but she had more than helped elevate his social standing.

Plus, of course, she was getting a weekend in Venice out of it for starters. Much more of a problem was this polenta stuff. It didn't taste anything like porridge. It was like baby food. She found herself laughing at the idea, nevertheless – Charlie saddled with another couple of brats, for life. It was hysterical.

'It's nothing like porridge, Charlie,' she said. 'What does it really remind you of?'

'Thrush,' he said. 'A bush full of thrush.'

The bar in the Gritti Palace was everything a bar should be, Charlie thought. Big, comfy antique chairs and sofas, cigar smoke, soft lighting, a guy on a piano, but not singing, glamorous women showing lots of leg. It was past 11, and Charlie was on his second brandy, Dorothy on her first whisky, but nearly having finished it.

'We've got a lot of ground to cover tomorrow, Charlie,' she said. 'We hardly saw anything today.'

'One Titian, you've seen them all,' Charlie said.

'We haven't seen any Tintorettos yet. Or any Bellinis.'

'That reminds me,' said Charlie. 'Harry's Bar. We could stop in there for a mid-morning pick-me-up.'

'I'm going to bed,' said Dorothy, standing. 'If you want a place to sleep tonight, I suggest you hurry up.'

'I'll just finish this, old girl. I'll be up in a jiffy.'

Charlie had no intention of being up in a jiffy. It wasn't even midnight, and how often was he in Venice? Besides, what he was hoping was that one or two of the glamorous-looking women showing lots of leg in the bar would actually be high-class hookers and that at the very least he'd be able to negotiate a first-class blow job in the toilets, and a bit of a grope. He knew it would probably be astronomically expensive – like everything else in the damned city – but then he'd always believed that in this world you had to pay for anything worthwhile. Nothing decent came for free.

Having watched Dorothy's large arse disappear in the lift, he started to look around the room properly. The two women who he thought were most likely to be on the game were chatting to three Americans. Charlie could tell that there were no couples in the grouping by their body language – the way the women were relating to each other, and then the men. The men were being much more reserved. Or two of them were. One wasn't. The loudest, and fattest, who was also the only one smoking a cigar.

If the women weren't hookers, Charlie thought, they were certainly up for it. The more he studied them, the more he realised that they weren't quite so glamorous but rather tarty – which, as far as he was concerned, was even more of a turn-on. Both were wearing bras which lifted their tits beautifully and gave them cleavages. And both were wearing sleeveless black dresses – one with red trimming, the other none. What Charlie couldn't tell, because they were sitting, was the exact shape of either of their behinds, and what shape their knickers made, if they were wearing any.

He loved looking out for VPLs, or a lack of a VPL.

Charlie was an arse man and he loved doing it doggy style. That's what had originally attracted him to Dorothy, her arse and the way she'd happily let him go at it like a Jack Russell, in fact just like their first Jack Russell, Jack, which they couldn't let anywhere near a bitch on heat. He was a total dog.

Except over the years, the decades, Dorothy's derrière had swelled and sagged immeasurably. Charlie still tried to give it a good poking every now and then, but it wasn't as firm, as tight, as neat, as Janet's, for example. Or, he presumed, either of the two hookers' being chatted up by the three Americans.

Charlie couldn't understand what three male Americans would be doing in the Gritti Palace, in Venice, on a Friday evening in June. He thought Venice was a place for couples, for romantic breaks, not for business trips, and these men looked like they were in town on business – chatting up a couple of hookers, who Charlie, becoming increasingly desperate, wanted to be chatting up himself. At least organising a rendezvous with in the toilet. He was never one to dawdle, when the possibility of sex was on offer.

The piano player thought he was the piano player out of *Casablanca*, thought Charlie. Perhaps he was. Looking around the quietly lit room, Charlie wondered whether there were any other options.

There weren't. All the other women – there were just three – were clearly with the people they were with. Blast, he said to himself, sinking the remains of his brandy, looking at his watch, looking at the high-class hookers and the Americans, seeing they seemed to be more entrenched than ever, realising his options were fast running out, and thinking that he'd spent two bloody grand on this trip, for what? The least he deserved was a fuck out of the old girl.

So he stood up, sensed he was a little more pissed than he thought he was, and headed for the lift, half hoping that one of the hookers would notice him and make a dash for it too, eager to top up her earnings, but one of them didn't, and he found himself going up to the fourth floor in the lift on his own.

The room was a junior suite, with a Grand Canal view. Heavy on the chintz, light on the atmosphere – and it was nearly half a grand a night. Dorothy was still awake, lying in bed reading *Riders*, her face glistening with moisturiser. 'Well, that's a surprise,' she said, not looking up from her book. 'Did the bar suddenly empty out?'

'I was missing you,' Charlie said. 'Couldn't stand the idea of you being up here all on your own. What?'

Coughing – any form of endearment, even if it was ironic, made him embarrassed – he walked over to one of the large windows and, pulling apart the thick curtains, stared down at the Grand Canal. Lights from the Gritti Palace itself and the surrounding palazzos were reflected on the calm black water. He didn't open the window, because the air-conditioning was on and he knew how hot and muggy, and smelly, it was outside.

And inside, under the covers, hopefully. He loved the smell of a woman in bed, playing with herself.

Throwing his blazer off, he moved over to the foot of the bed. Removing his shoes, unsteadily, he untucked the bottom of the sheets and started to crawl up the inside of the bed, quickly coming across Dorothy's bare legs, which he roughly parted, and now crawling up the inside of her nightie too, he headed straight for her bush, parting her legs more – indeed, as much as her nightie would allow.

'Charlie,' he heard her say, but muffled because he was in a chintzy room and under so many covers, and his ears were being blocked by the insides of her fat white thighs, 'I'm reading. Jilly Cooper.'

'Carry on,' he said, between mouthfuls of pubic hair. 'Don't mind me.'

Not many moments later, he had a better idea. Pulling back

his head and having wiped his mouth on one of his wife's thighs, he said, 'Actually, Dotty, could you turn over? It's bloody hot and cramped under here.'

Because Dorothy had been reading Jilly Cooper, a particularly steamy scene in a stable, she hadn't minded Charlie foraging between her legs. Apart from anything else, it was an extremely rare occurrence. So, knowing full well what would be coming if she did turn over, she turned over happily enough, hauling her nightie higher up and over her bottom. She managed to keep *Riders* open at the right page and, propping a pillow under her chest, and lifting her bottom off the bed and into the air, though it was still a bit constricted by the top sheet, she carried on reading, riveted to know whether Rupert would finally get his end away with Fen, in the stable, or not.

Having got rid of the top sheet, Charlie was inside her and starting to go at it like Jack, before Dorothy had reached the bottom of the page. Even Charlie was pleased with the swiftness with which he found himself fucking Dotty, doggy style. As far as he could remember it was the first time they'd done it since she'd found out about Janet. Aside from the swiftness, he was also pleased that Dotty hadn't gone on about Janet, hadn't tried to make him feel guilty about all that – she really was a brick, his wife. And he was even pleased that he wasn't in some toilet, however clean and plush one of the Gritti Palace's public toilets might have been, getting a blow job off an overpriced hooker.

He was enjoying taking his wife from behind, enjoying her dark, slippery grand canal. But getting into a rhythm, hearing himself slap against her backside, and the sloshing of her fanny juices as he bashed away – such a Venetian sound, Charlie couldn't help thinking – he was becoming more and more aware that Dorothy was not Janet. However homely he found Dotty, her large, saggy but usually always welcoming rear, she just wasn't Janet. He missed the firmness, the shapeliness, the tautness of his mistress's arse. And the high-pitched yelp she made when she came. Which was only all the fucking time.

Grand Canal, Once More, Please, Quickly

It felt good to be back, so to speak. Except we were not back, we were away, for once. What a treat that was.

I was on the bed – and what a bed, what sheets, what extra-fine Egyptian cotton – on all fours, with Charlie going at it with his usual vigour from behind. He loved that position. I didn't mind it, though I was not so keen when he tried to pull my bum apart so he could get a better look or something. He was not doing that then. He was just bashing away, with his hands on my upper back – not even on my tits. Sometimes he used to lean forward a bit more and cup my breasts, and tweak my nipples with his fingers, but right then he was simply making love to me, fast, almost furiously – making up for lost time, for the fact that we hadn't done it for months and months, for the fact that he'd behaved so bloody monstrously, so I thought, probably misguidedly.

Also he was a little pissed. And when Charlie was pissed, usually he could only concentrate on one particular thing. Like fucking me. Invariably, he couldn't be bothered to play with my nipples at the same time, or reach around and gently stroke my clitoris, while he was bashing away.

What used to happen, when he was pissed, was that once he'd decided he was coming to bed – I was usually in it by then – he'd suddenly rip his clothes off, untuck the sheets and get in from the bottom, climbing up the bed, and up me. He might attempt a bit of cunnilingus, for no more than thirty seconds or so. He had a very rough tongue, and his nose always seemed to get in the way. Actually, it was bit like he was fucking me with his nose. Most peculiar.

Anyway, soon enough he'd say something like, 'Can you turn over? It's bloody hot and cramped down here.' And I'd turn over happily enough. Quite frankly it was always a bit of a relief. I can tell you, you'd rather be fucked by Charlie's penis than his nose any day. Once turned over, I'd raise my bum a little, or just get on to all fours, and before I knew it Charlie would have entered me, and be bashing away, his usual puce, cheerful self.

The good thing was he always took ages to come, especially if he were pissed. More than ample time for me to have a go myself. Because, I suppose, more often than not Charlie was pissed, and if he were taking me from behind he'd be pretty much concentrating on that, just bashing away, his hands on my upper back for support, leaving the front of my vagina where it counts completely untouched. There was obviously no way I was going to reach orgasm like that, so while he was bashing away, almost forgetting about me, I'd try to prop myself on one elbow, or just sort of reach under with my right hand, and play with myself.

I enjoyed it. I liked feeling Charlie's penis sliding in and out of me, while I drew little circles with my finger on my clitoris. Round and round I went. It was nice being so wet, and I liked the way his penis would pull and distend my labia, and how I could feel with my fingers his hard, wet shaft moving in and out. Plus, in this position I could always tell when Charlie was about to come. He'd suddenly increase the tempo, stop for a few seconds, breathing heavily, then plunge in again, stop once more, then make a third, final dash for it. Normally.

That time, on those beautiful sheets, on that sumptuous bed, in that luxurious room with a quite stunning view of the Grand Canal – oh, he'd pulled out all the stops, all right – he didn't come on the third, final dash.

I did, however. Just before I came I stopped gently circling my clitoris and pinched it, hard, between my thumb and forefinger. I had a lovely orgasm and might even have yelped a bit. I did that when I came. Collapsing after, because I could no longer support myself, let alone Charlie, I felt Charlie slide out of me, his penis still hard. Then Charlie was lying flat on top of me, his penis wedged between my bum cheeks. For a short while he attempted to fuck me like that, sort of rubbing his penis between my bottom, but he quickly gave up.

For once, I thought, he'd actually had too much to drink. Though I'd come, it still felt like a bit of a shame he hadn't, seeing as he'd brought me all the way to Venice, to this absolutely spectacular hotel. I'm not saying I didn't deserve it, after the way he had treated me and our children – it was the first proper break I'd had from them – but nevertheless I felt sorry for him at that moment.

It was his fault, of course. He'd insisted on having a nightcap in the bar after dinner. I don't particularly blame him for that. It was a lovely bar, softly lit, stuffed with antique furniture, and there was this piano player, an old black man, who, of course, reminded me of Sam in *Casablanca*. And there were all these very glamorous people. A couple of particularly gorgeous women, in short, tight black dresses and wearing lots of jewellery, who, if they hadn't been sitting where they were, and in that hotel, and with the people they were with, I might have mistaken for high-class prostitutes. Charlie, of course, couldn't keep his eyes off them. But I didn't mind. Charlie was Charlie. He was always attracted to good-looking, sexy young women, which in a way only ever made me feel better about myself. He wouldn't have been with me had he not found me attractive. Would he?

He had two brandies, at least, before I decided to go up to the room. I wasn't paying attention to how much he had to drink over dinner. For such an impressive hotel, with such a gloriously attractive restaurant, with a terrace right on the Grand Canal, lit by oil lamps, the food was not great, there was too much of this weird polenta stuff, a bit like porridge, at least that was what Charlie thought. I didn't. It was nothing like porridge. I happen to like porridge. Anyway, I probably drank more than normal, trying to take the taste away, so I'm not sure how much Charlie actually had. We had more than one bottle, that was for sure.

In the bar I felt someone had to initiate something. I mean, it seemed such a shame that we'd come all the way to Venice, to the most romantic city in the world, even if it was because Charlie had behaved appallingly and was trying to make up to me, and not have had one tiny little screw yet.

I told Charlie I was going to the room. 'Don't be long,' I said, giving him one of my looks.

He wasn't as long as I had expected. I had barely time to get undressed and into my nightie – I had brought one specially – and into bed. It was a gorgeous bed, as wide as it was long. A bed made for passionate sex.

But Charlie couldn't come. He lay there, on top of me, his penis resting between my bum, beginning to go floppy. I reached behind my back and between our bodies and took hold of it for a minute or two, trying to squeeze some life into it. It was getting more limp and floppy by the second.

'It's not working, Janet. I'm sorry,' he said.

'You can do that thing, if you like,' I said. 'That thing' was when he tried to poke his penis up my arsehole, but he never got very far, thank God, and after a bit of rather painful prodding would stick it where it was meant to go. 'Or that other thing,' I said. 'That other thing' was when he sort of sat on top of me and stuck his penis between my breasts and tried to fuck me like that. I think he called it titty fucking.

'I don't think either would work,' he said. 'It's most peculiar. The last time I was here, with the old girl, I didn't have any problems.'

'What?' I said. 'When the fucking hell was that?' He'd never mentioned he'd been to Venice with his wife, though I had presumed he'd been to Venice some time before. He sort of knew his way around, and seemed to know the hotel a bit too.

'I can't remember,' he said. 'A few months ago.'

'A few months ago?' I had managed to push him off me by now and was sitting up in that wonderful bed. 'A few months ago?'

'Maybe it was longer ago than that,' he said. 'But don't you just love the Grand Canal? I can't get it out of my mind. The Grand Canal. That's what I want. Hey, hang on a minute. Something's going on.'

Pulling back what was left of the sheets, Charlie showed me his penis. It was becoming erect again, all on its own.

'How did that happen?' I said.

'Don't know. Mind over matter. Anyway, Janet,' he said, putting his arm across my chest, a hand on my breast, his other hand between my legs, 'we might as well make use of it, don't you reckon? Can we try once more, please, quickly?'

'No,' I said, and from then on I kept saying no. And I meant it.

Part Four
Betrayal, Knickerbox, £10

Arrivals

'Brian, Brian,' says Sally, 'there it is. I think.'

'That's not it,' Brian says. 'Ours is bigger. And it doesn't have a blue handle.'

'Is that it?' she says, pointing.

'That one? Don't be an idiot.'

They are by the luggage carousel, Palma Airport. It's heaving, but Brian managed to push his way to the front line, dragging Sally with him. He hates queuing and he hates crowds and he hates airports and he hates going abroad and he particularly hates Sally's father Charlie and he can't understand why the hell they have come all this way at such enormous expense just for the old boy's birthday even if he's going to be seventy and is about to peg it by all accounts.

'No, that's not the bag either,' he says, seeing Sally fixing on yet another piece of someone else's luggage trundling along the ludicrously slow luggage carousel. The slowest he's ever seen. Though he supposes that that might have something to do with the fact that it's so laden. He can't believe there's just one planeload of luggage going round and round.

There are children everywhere and hideously fat grown-ups, and for some strange reason lots of Spanish policemen or customs officials, with dogs and machine guns. And Brian can't believe the vast luggage reclaim hall is air-conditioned. It is absolutely fucking boiling and it's only 10.30 or something in the morning local time. Their plane from Gatwick left at 6.50. Well, it was meant to. It actually left at least half an hour later. Brian was trying not to pay attention, to the time, or the noise coming from the baby in the row behind and the baby's parents arguing about how to shut the brat up. Or the prospect of a week in Majorca with his in-laws. He doesn't know how he let Sally talk him into it. Especially as it's not even free. It's costing a fortune. And he's paying every fucking penny because Sally's still fucking redundant.

No wonder, he thinks. She can't even remember which is her own luggage.

It's starting to smell, being so packed in. With all these people and children jostling by the carousel, and tempers beginning to fray, because the carousel is absolutely overflowing with luggage – endless suitcases and extra-large holdalls and the odd car seat and pushchair and bags of golf clubs and more suitcases, those huge ones with wheels, cardboard boxes bound up with tape and string and the odd kid larking about going round with it – but nobody is picking anything off.

'It's the wrong one,' says Brian. 'I bet we're waiting at the wrong fucking carousel.'

'It says it's the right one,' says Sally. She's feeling exhausted. And hot and clammy and very uncomfortable in her jeans and sweatshirt. She hadn't intended to wear her jeans or her sweatshirt. She had laid out a light summer dress and cardigan, ready for the early start. But it was freezing when they got up, and still almost dark, so she put on what she had been wearing yesterday – clothes she had spent the day in cleaning up and packing and watering the garden and getting everything ready.

'I don't understand how people can take so much stuff with them,' Brian says. 'It defies me.'

Sally needs a pee. She should have gone on the plane, before it landed, but she was so wedged in she couldn't be bothered. Also, she had a bikini wax yesterday morning and apart from the fact that they seem to have pulled off more than she asked for – Christ, she's almost bald down there – it still stings when she pees, so she's trying to go as little as possible.

She's still not sure why she got it done. A few weeks ago she was determined she was never going to have another bikini wax in her life. Or wear skimpy knickers and thongs, and swimsuits, of course. Since she was made redundant early in the spring she had grown used to wearing sloppy clothes and being unkempt and letting everything grow in the way nature intended – her bush, as well as the garden. It made her feel strangely sexy. As if she were more in tune with her body, her needs. And not pandering to some idea of who she should be, not pandering to fashion.

But when she went shopping for a new swimsuit in M&S last week she found herself in the lingerie department and she couldn't believe how the ranges had improved. Which made her realise quite how long it had been since she'd bought any underwear, and exactly what sort of state her present stuff was in. And she was also reminded of that ludicrous afternoon at Lin and Owen's, her neighbours, when they were all extremely drunk, and for some reason decided to show each other what knickers they were wearing. And Lin, of fucking course, was wearing a very skimpy, pretty much totally see-through thong, from M&S, so she said. Brian couldn't stop staring.

At the time Sally thought, What a tart. Typical. Then she forgot about it. Then she found herself in M&S, wandering around the massive lingerie bit, and she spotted the thong Lin had been wearing. The exact same one, from a label called Truly You. With see-through black material on the front edged in pink. Not really thinking, she put a size twelve in her basket. She's really a size fourteen, but she finds with thongs it doesn't make much difference to how comfortable they are whether you go down a size, they are always agony. However, psychologically it makes an enormous amount of difference to her whether she buys a size twelve or a size fourteen.

She put a bikini in too. And then went back to the lingerie bit and put in other size twelve Truly You thongs and size thirty-six C bras, in different colour coordinations. Thinking that she might as well go the whole hog. Why, exactly, she's still not sure.

'See,' says Brian. 'I fucking knew it.' He's spotted a change in the flight details above their carousel – along with everyone else. They have been waiting at the wrong one, or at least the people in charge got it wrong. The luggage which has spewed out and is going round and round endlessly appears to be from a flight from Hamburg. 'That fucking explains it,' says Brian. 'Who else would need so much luggage?'

Brian hasn't spotted any of his in-laws yet. They had heard that Sally's half-sister Alicia, and her new boyfriend, were on the same easyJet flight. But there's been no sign of them so far. Sally's father and mother are coming tomorrow. Her sister Catherine and her kids, and even apparently Catherine's weird ex-husband, tomorrow also. Brian doesn't know why they had to get there so early.

'We should be at that one,' says Sally. 'Number eight.'

'I can read too,' Brian shouts, beginning to break into a trot, not bothering to see whether Sally is following. They are hiring a car, once they've got their luggage, and he knows how long the queue will be if he's not at the Autos Serra desk quick enough. This is the last time I go away in August, he's thinking, reaching the new carousel, which is not just empty, it's not even going round.

Sally is on her way to the toilet, thinking, Why do I put up with him? She's hotter than ever and itchy in all the wrong places and hugely tired and absolutely bursting for a pee. The toilet is miles away. Right across the hall with the luggage carousels – there must be at least fifteen of the things, most of them crowded with people – and along a wide corridor and down a flight of stairs and around a corner. She doesn't know whether she'll ever find her way back to Brian. Not that she cares particularly.

And waiting inside the toilet for a free cubicle – she can't believe that there's a queue even here, deep in the bowels of the airport, miles from anywhere – she begins to imagine what would happen if, when she's had her pee, she leaves the toilet and, going back upstairs, hooks up with a different husband, waiting at another carousel, and slips into a totally different holiday, and life, with a job, perhaps, and children, maybe, and a decent, fulfilling sex life. Effectively, she wonders what it would be like to be attached to a man she fancied for once, rather than someone she puts up with, and shags very occasionally just to prove to herself that she can still do it and hasn't totally dried up.

A cubicle comes free, and Sally rushes for it. She really is bursting and she rips at the stud button on her jeans and the buttons on the fly and shoves them down, with her knickers at the same time, and hovering over the toilet – she never actually sits on a public toilet seat unless she really has to – she pees and pees. But because of the angle she's hovering at she can feel pee getting on to her almost-hairless pubic mound and the raw skin there stings like mad.

Having wiped herself thoroughly, which only makes it worse, she pulls up her knickers and her jeans, still cross with the salon for tearing off more than was reasonable, far more than is decent, and cross with herself for bothering to have had a bikini wax in the first place. She's thirty-nine. She's been married for what feels like for ever. She's bored rigid with Brian. She's bored with not having a job. With not having children. With not having a sex life, to speak of. Why is she so bothered with what she looks like in a bikini?

But what if, she's thinking, when I leave the toilet, and walk all those miles back upstairs, everything is different, and I'm hooked up with another chap? Someone new and exciting and outrageously sexy, waiting at a different carousel, because I will have just jetted in not from Gatwick, but Hamburg say, or, or, she doesn't know where, but somewhere more exciting than south London anyway. And this outrageously sexy man, a German, perhaps – well, she thinks, what's wrong with Germans? She likes them. She thinks they always look clean, and well built, and really rather randy too – will be about to whisk me off to some fancy hotel, bang on the sea.

The first thing they'll do, once they've checked in, once they've got to the room, will be to strip off and shag. The sort of shag that seems like it goes on for ever but actually lasts only a couple of minutes as it's all so new and you are so heated. With lots of very athletic movements and interesting positions – because in this alternative reality Sally will be fit and lean – and with lots of Germanic grunting also. She likes that idea. Letting off steam, years of it.

Reaching the vast carousel concourse, even more crowded and confused than before, Sally starts wondering why she's become so obsessed with sex. And with trying to change her life. Actually, with wanting to live a different life. All summer she's been confused about who she is and just what she wants. Moving from a restrained, cowed, redundant woman, to something more wild and earthy and determined – but still not truly herself. Now, with her new bikini wax and her suitcase full of skimpy lingerie, and a very high-cut bikini too – almost a total reversal of who she was before she was made redundant, at least – for her week in Majorca, she's no more sure of herself. At least, she's no more sure of who she wants to be with.

Surely she didn't get kitted out for Brian, she's thinking, approaching carousel eight. What a waste, if that were the case. Surely it's time to move on.

'Where the fuck have you been?' Brian says, grabbing Sally's arm, pulling her to the front line. 'The luggage is finally coming round. You could have missed it.'

'Yeah, but you wouldn't have,' she says. 'That's why you've been waiting here, while I've been looking for the toilet. It was miles away.' She doesn't know why she's making excuses. So what if she took ages? Their luggage hasn't even appeared.

'This place is a nightmare,' Brian says. 'I don't know why we're here. We shouldn't have come. The whole week is going to be fucking awful.' He's so annoyed about the situation he can't think clearly. His mind is thick and red and hot. 'Why can't something go right for once?' he's saying, not listening to Sally.

Who's saying, 'Why do I have to put up with you? Why can't I be with someone new? Anyone. Him, for instance.' Standing just to her left is, she quickly decides, a very good-looking young man. He's nearly six feet, lean but fit-looking, with neat dark-brown hair. He's wearing sunglasses, pushed back on his head, a light, short-sleeved summer shirt, loose jeans and sandals. To Sally he looks remarkably relaxed and rather cool, and dead sexy. Also, he's looking at her, in more than a casual, accidental way.

He can't be interested in me, she's thinking. He can't be checking me out. Surely? And to have spotted him in this crowd. To be standing almost next to him. Or is he the answer to my dreams? A way out of here. Has he been sent by God?

'Sally?' Alicia says. 'Is it you?'

Emerging from behind the man comes Alicia, Sally's half-sister. Neither has seen the other for years.

'Alicia?' Sally says.

'Hi,' Alicia says. 'It's me.'

Sally can't believe how gorgeous her half-sister looks. She is so trim, in her short denim skirt and tiny white T-shirt, and she has such lovely skin, and brunette-coloured hair. She also has sunglasses pushed back on her head, holding her hair back, and revealing even more of her beautiful face. Sally's beginning to wonder about exactly what genes they have in common.

'This is Mikey,' Alicia says. 'Mikey, this is Sally.'

Mikey holds out his hand and, winking, says, 'I've heard all about you.' He hasn't, but that's what he always says when he meets Alicia's friends and family.

Sally says, looking the other way but not seeing her husband, 'Brian's here somewhere. Brian?'

'Sally,' she hears, 'where the fuck have you got to now?' It's Brian. 'It's finally fucking coming. Give us a hand.'

The next thing Sally knows is that Brian's holdall lands at her feet. Brian's flung it there. She looks at Alicia and Mikey, who both seem so calm and cool, and sexy, despite the early hour and all the travelling they must have just done, and the terrible surroundings of the carousel concourse at Palma Airport. She wishes she looked a little more decent, and sexy, herself. She feels so shy, and plain, and ugly. And unloved.

'Fuck it,' says Brian, shoving their main, hard-shell suitcase across to Sally. There are so many people by the edge of the carousel he can barely manoeuvre it. Being so hot and cross and fed up already, he doesn't realise quite how hard he shoves it, but it really flies into a fully loaded trolley, narrowly missing two young children and a baby in a pushchair.

Sally is not sure whether it was the force with which Brian shoved it or whether it just caught the trolley at an odd angle, but the lid springs open and, with the suitcase coming to rest on its side, heaps of clothes spill out on to the shiny concourse floor. Sally always packs way too much – Brian's stuff at the bottom, hers at the top, because she doesn't like hers to be too creased, and Brian doesn't care.

Except this time Sally wishes she'd packed her stuff at the bottom, as they are clearly her clothes that are all over the floor. Starting with the light summer dress and cardigan she had intended to wear, closely followed by – oh God, she realises – her new Truly You M&S underwear.

Everyone is looking.

Most of the underwear is in a frilly heap, but one thong, the Truly You one, with see-through black material on the front edged in pink, is lying on the floor, on its back, all on its own.

Brian doesn't know where it's come from. As usual, he played no part in the packing. He thinks it looks vaguely familiar, but he's sure he's never seen such an item on his wife. Besides, the last time he looked, his wife's bush was so wild and unkempt he can't begin to imagine how she'd wear such a thing – the days when she wore underwear like that were over months, years ago, he thinks. Indeed, he half wonders whether someone else might have dropped it.

However, this is the first piece of underwear Sally rushes to retrieve. Picking it up, she crunches it in her hand, trying to make it disappear. No one, not even Brian, has exactly come to her aid, she's pleased to discover, though looking around she sees that Alicia and Mikey are not only staring at her and her most intimate things, like everyone else, but have shuffled over so they are sort of standing guard over the opened suitcase and its spilled contents.

'Let me help,' says Alicia, crouching also.

Looking at all the new underwear, realising the thong does indeed belong to his wife, Brian's mood rapidly improves. Fuck me, he thinks, this holiday might just be all right. 'At least we've got the luggage,' he says, 'and it hasn't been mixed up and sent to Hamburg or wherever. You hear about that happening all the time.' He can't wait to get his hands on Sally in this stuff.

Seeing Brian look at her things and the look he's giving her, Sally says, 'Don't get any ideas, Brian. It's not for you.'

'What?' Brian says.

'Nice underwear, Sally,' Alicia says, trying to laugh. Trying to make it sound like a joke. Trying to lighten the atmosphere.

'Are we all staying in the same hotel?' Mikey says, looking at Sally.

Jesus

Done, I'm thinking. Already. Because guess who's taking me out tonight? Can you believe it?

Jesus.

I'm such a slapper.

What's more, I still haven't exactly dumped Pedro either. He's at a Seat freebie in Barcelona. Gone for forty-eight hours.

'Pedro,' I said, 'how can you do this to me?'

'Zara,' he said, in that thick accent of his, 'you'll be all right. You can amuse yourself, my little darling.' His English might be getting better, but he's lost the plot as far as I'm concerned.

'But Kim's busy, and none of my family are here yet, and work's like really slow at the moment, and I'm feeling really hot.' I winked at him when I said that. I lied also. Kim wasn't busy and some of my family had arrived, though none of the ones I like, but work was really slow – the hotel's been under half-full since the stomach bug hit in July. Loads of punters have cancelled, which was why my family managed to get in.

By all accounts, with a pretty amazing deal. They are so cheap.

'Play with yourself,' he said. 'It's two nights.'

'I need to be entertained,' I said. 'I hate being on my own.'

'That's your problem,' he said.

Of course it's his problem, because the morning he flew off to Barcelona I happened to find myself wandering down by the marina, where they keep all the Sunseekers, and who should I bump into, driving along a jetty on his moped, with his shoulder-length hair blowing in the wind, his white shirt billowing, his faded shorts pressed tight against his deeply tanned thighs, his dusty leather sandals on the pedals, but Jesus.

'Hi,' I said, as he slowed to a wobble before putting his dusty sandalled feet down on the wooden jetty. I'm not sure whether I noticed them before, but Jesus does have lovely legs.

'Zara,' he said. 'What you doing here?'

'Looking for you,' I joked. Except it wasn't a joke.

'Well, you have found me,' he joked back.

I was wearing my denim shorts, not Kim's, which I think are like really 1980s, or is it 1970s? You know, what's her name, Farrah Fawcett from *Charlie's Angels*, the original one – the sort of thing she would wear. They are frayed at the ends; in fact, they are so frayed they are more fray than denim. Plus they are so tight in the crotch they almost split me in two. I can't walk far in them. But I can't walk far in my platform espadrilles, either. Have you ever tried walking in platform espadrilles? They have these ties which wrap around your ankles and then calves, which are meant to support you, but they don't, they just cut off your circulation. And the espadrille bit, the bit you put you feet into and stand on, these layers of matting, squidge this way and that as you walk. Except when it's wet, then they are like bricks. Actually paving slabs. And they stink.

Casually putting my hand on his handlebars for support, and gently rubbing my left shin with my right espadrille – except it wasn't gentle, it scratched – I said, 'Fancy taking me for a ride?' He must have known I was chatting him up.

'On this thing?' he said, looking down at his moped, looking at me in my very short, very frayed shorts. Looking straight at my crotch.

'No,' I said, pointing to the row of gleaming speedboats moored to the jetty, 'in one of those.'

'That's not possible today,' he said. 'I have to work.'

'Later?' I said.

'What you doing later?' he said in a slightly strange, slightly suspicious voice, I thought, which might have been his way of saying, What's happened to Pedro? But he didn't mention his best friend's name. He must have know he was in Barcelona.

'What are you offering?' I said.

'A friend of mine, he has a new bar. It's opening tonight,' he said. 'I'll pick you up at your hotel,' he said. 'The Gran Sol, yes?'

'That's the one,' I said, thinking he's even more presumptuous than me. 'Where everyone's been sick.' I laughed.

So here I am, nearly ready, waiting for Jesus.

I thought I'd try out the frock I'm going to wear for Dad's party on Friday. It's short and black, of course, and I picked it up in H&M before I left the UK. It's the poshest frock I have with me. And get this: I'm wearing my poshest underwear too. It's also black, though that sort of semi-see-through material, and edged with pink. My bra and my thong, they match for once. But the funniest thing is the set's called Betrayal. I bought it in Knickerbox, also before I left the UK, and I've been saving it for a special occasion. I thought Dad's do would be the night, but how could I resist getting it out early?

Jesus, I'm thinking, are you in for a pleasant surprise. The last time he saw me, apart from this morning, of course, was when he took Pedro and me out on a Sunseeker, and I was like either just in my silver bikini bottoms or totally fucking naked – no, nothing did go on. It got close, but that was it.

I might be a right slapper, but I do believe in a little modesty now and then. As long as it's classy, and this Betrayal gear certainly looks that.

To be honest, waiting here all togged up, with my slap on, I'm suddenly feeling a little nervous. It's not because I feel guilty about Pedro or anything, but Jesus is late and I'm not totally sure what I think about him – now he's about to show, now he better fucking show. The way he was behaving that day on the boat with Pedro, I thought he was like really gay. But since, I'm not so sure. It's probably just the way Spanish men are, because Pedro can seem a bit gay, especially when we're having sex and he tries to ram his fat penis up my arsehole.

I have this friend back home, Julie, who thinks that it's only men with small dicks who insist on having anal sex, and those who are secretly gay, of course. Pedro doesn't have a small dick. As you know, it's not massively long, but it's fucking fat. He might, though, be a bit gay. Like Jesus. Or it might just be a Spanish thing.

Take Spanish footballers. They are not exactly the most macho-looking blokes I've ever seen on a pitch. Or Enriques Iglesias. Look at him. He's camper than George Michael. So what if he just married that female tennis player? They're all dykes anyway, aren't they?

Still, Jesus is taking me out tonight, so how can he be gay?

Also, I'm a little nervous about his beard. I've never been with a bloke with a beard before. Stubble, yeah. But not a proper beard. I mean, just how much does it itch? Lots of men, some very eminent ones, have beards, don't they? They can't all have total dogs for girlfriends. Who's the most famous I can think of? Father Christmas. Well, he obviously doesn't have much of a partner. Richard Branson. Don't know about his wife, but I very nearly applied to Virgin for a job, before I spotted the ad for Majorcan Dreams. Can you imagine, me as a hostie?

I did think, when I first met Jesus, that he'd be really gorgeous without a beard. That that would be the first thing I'd insist had to go – if we, rather when we became an item. But I'm not so sure now. It can't be that painful, can it? Or ticklish? And it's not just the snogging I'm thinking about. What's it like having some man with a beard go down on you?

Guess what? I'm about to find out.

So this is how the evening has gone so far.

Jesus was forty minutes late, which I reckon for a Spaniard is like being early. He turns up wearing a pair of loose white trousers, those dusty sandals, but he's given them a rub, and a white shirt. He'd obviously had a shower because his hair was soft and shiny, as was his beard. It all sort of flowed and swayed around him, and if I was not determined to think otherwise I would have sworn he looked about as camp as any punter I've ever seen. But I was determined to think otherwise, and in that frame of mind I thought he just looked absolutely fucking gorgeous, dead sexy and very, very macho, in a Spanish sort of way.

Any nervousness or inhibitions I'd had earlier about the beard suddenly flew out of the window, except that wasn't quite what happened because my room, the room I share with Kim, doesn't have a window. However, the beard looked all right. It fitted in. It was part and parcel.

He came up and kissed me, on the lips, and I immediately felt totally at ease with him, even proud to be with him. Because in his way, if you can accept the get-up and the beard, he's a pretty good-looking fella, and clearly has a touch more class than Pedro. Well, he's in the motorboat business, isn't he? Not the fucking sleazy car-hire business.

Leaving the Gran Sol – no, we didn't shag immediately, no, I didn't run my hands through that beard, that kiss on the lips was it, for then – we walked round to the front of the hotel, in view of everyone, not that I'm sure anyone was looking. But how I wanted to be seen, by my colleagues, by the punters, what few there were, by the odd, distant member of my family hanging out on a balcony. Because on the street, bang in front of the Gran Sol, Jesus motioned towards this gleaming sports car – a silver two-seater Merc. Top of the range, latest model. With the top down, of course.

'Tonight,' he said, 'we drive.'

'Where did you get this?' I said.

'I have friends in the car business,' he said, winking.

So does Pedro, I thought, but he never picked me up in a Merc.

Even getting in was a laugh. Have you ever got into such a low-slung thing in a tight black dress? By the time I was sitting comfortably it was practically around my waist. But I didn't care because I was wearing my flashy, pink and black Betrayal thong. It was like, get an eyeful of that, Jesus.

Pure class, I thought as we zoomed off, Robbie Williams's 'Let Me Entertain You' booming on the sound system.

To be honest, Jesus' mate's new bar was bit of a dive. It was in Port de Pollenca, on the front, but at the far end, away from the main drag. I don't know who it's meant to appeal to. Tourists, or locals.

Tonight it was definitely for locals, which I suppose is not surprising. Jesus knew everyone, of course. What's more, loads of the blokes had beards. It was so weird, as if they were all members of a club. The beardies' club. I'm not really sure why Jesus took me, as he chatted away in Spanish to everyone. He did introduce me to people, however, and pretty much kept his hand on my back the whole time – guiding me around, and now and then letting his hand slip over my arse. Perhaps he was just showing me off. Perhaps he was saying,

Look everyone, look who I've pulled. See, I'm not really gay. Who knows?

We might not have said much to each other throughout the evening – the music was terrible too; the Spanish just don't get it – but by the time we got back in the Merc we were all over each other. Robbie Williams came on like magic – 'No Regrets' – and Jesus had his hand between my legs, his fingers fishing beneath my thong, well before we'd gone anywhere.

Because I was dripping, and he clearly knew his way around a girl's bits and bobs, I was sort of concentrating on that, and not on the kissing front, though I have to say a guy with a beard is a lot more comfortable to snog than a guy with stubble. While a beard might tickle, at least it's soft. Stubble just scratches like shit. I didn't come in the car. You want to know a secret? I've never come in a car. I think I must be from a different generation. All the people I know who've had proper sex in cars are really ancient.

I had to squeeze my legs shut, push his head away, and say, 'Jesus, can we go somewhere a bit more comfortable? Nice as this car is.' I was hoping he'd drive me to a Sunseeker. Even that Portofino 35 he took Pedro and me on the other week. But no.

He said, 'Yes, Zara, we do that.' His English suddenly went as wonky as his driving, but we made it back to the Gran Sol in one piece, Jesus almost skidding to a halt bang outside the front again.

OK, I am a little disappointed he brought me back here so soon. Also Kim, my roommate, might turn up at any minute, though we have a code to warn each other that the room might be otherwise occupied. We leave our shoes outside the front door. I don't think Jesus even noticed me slipping off my fake Blahniks before we entered the room – he had his hands all over my tits.

Now he's pulling off my thong. I'm lying on the bed – Kim's, because it's more comfortable than mine – having already shed my dress and my bra, and my shoes, of course, so I'm down to the most intimate part of my Betrayal.

Apart from having taken off his sandals, Jesus is fully clothed. But for the moment I don't care about that. Not in the least.

He has his hands on either side of my thong, and as he tugs I lift my bum in the air, and it is halfway down my thighs, and I kick a bit, as he sits up to pull it the rest of the way off, and he's back between my legs, kissing and licking me, his soft beard brushing the soft skin of my inner thighs, and although it tickles like crazy it does feel great, in a very hairy way.

Of course, being cleanly shaved myself, it only feels weirder and hairier, like I can feel every hair on his face. As his tongue starts to probe inside me deeper and deeper, and he starts to munch away on my clit, and I can feel all this hair around me down there, it's like I've suddenly grown a massive bush – forgetting the head that's attached to it.

Obviously, it's not just the hair that is such a huge, strange turn-on. He clearly knows what he's doing with his mouth, his tongue, his teeth.

'Jesus,' I whisper, shutting my eyes, my mind drifting back to his mate's bar, and all the other beardies there. I need to tell Kim about this. Any babe who'll listen.

Either that, or I'm thinking, but not really thinking straight, because he's munching to a rhythm, putting me on the brink, so every nerve ending is like super-sensitive, and it just feels so hairy and wet down there, sort of wild in a way, primitive, pagan, even, so I'm thinking, but not, I should get a transplant, because I'm fucked if I'm going to wait for it to grow that long and bushy.

The Beach

'Hey,' says Mikey, 'come and look at this.'

Mikey's on the balcony, Alicia's in the toilet, but with the door open, finishing her make-up.

'Alicia,' he says, 'you've gotta come and see this.' Mikey's killing himself. It's the funniest thing he's seen for ages. Since CenterParcs, in fact.

'What?' Alicia says. She joins him on the balcony in her new, white string bikini, a Gucci rip-off, and her face perfectly made up. It will be her first day on the beach and she doesn't want to look like a total dog.

'There,' says Mikey, pointing and laughing.

'Where?' she says.

'Just beyond the pedalos.'

Alicia doesn't see anything. Or rather all she sees is a beach, people, pedalos, sea, and in the distance more sea and the sweep of the bay. It's slightly hazy, as if the heat, the mugginess hanging in the air, has become visible. Their hotel room is not air-conditioned, and is absolutely boiling, but out on the balcony, in direct hazy sunlight, it's even hotter. It's not quite 10 a.m.

'What am I meant to be looking at?' Alicia says, holding her hand to her forehead, trying to shade the sun. She doesn't know what she's done with her sunglasses.

Mikey's still killing himself, hanging on to the balcony rail, almost bent double. 'That fat, bald bloke,' he says. 'In a thong. He looks even more ludicrous than Bob. Remember? Bob at CenterParcs?'

'Him? There? That man? Coming this way? Fuck, that's what's-his-name, I'm sure,' Alicia says. 'You know, Catherine's ex. The one who went off with a bloke.'

Mark woke up at 6.30, couldn't get back to sleep because of the heat and the noise of a generator or extractor fan, or something with an engine nearby, so he lay sprawled on his bed until almost 9. He was thinking about Jacques mostly – he still misses him – and trying to remember what it was like before, when he was married to Catherine, and the last family holiday they'd gone on, which was, he seemed to think, probably the first too.

He was thinking about his kids, Jack, Toby and Victoria, who were in a room near their mother, in a different part of the hotel. He was thinking about their grandfather, and Catherine's dad, Charlie – the reason why they were all here. And how surprised he was really to have been invited to Charlie's seventieth. But the thing he always liked about the old boy was that he was never judgemental – at least, not about failed relationships or matters to do with one's libido. Because he understood just what could happen when things got out of hand.

Lying in bed, with the heat becoming more intense and the sweat beginning to pour from his body and soak the sheets, Mark couldn't help thinking about what a dreadful hotel it was, and how he worked his arse off, for what? To stay in a dump, without any air-conditioning. He could afford five-star luxury. He could afford the best. Indeed, lying there, he thought that there was no way he'd be able to last the week and would have to check into La Residencia.

But then he thought about his kids, off in another part of the same crappy hotel, having to cope with the heat and noise too, and he thought how seldom it was that he went abroad with them, at least found himself abroad with them, in the very same place, even if they were in another part of the same hotel, with their mother – indeed, under the very strict control of that woman.

He laughed to himself at that idea – strict, desperate Catherine, with her big arse all over the place – and continued laughing for a bit, at how sensitive she was about her figure, about having boyfriends, about maintaining an image, some sort of show for her neighbours, and her broader family, who certainly didn't care one way or another, because they were all bonkers when it came to the bed department. But then, he thought, at least she's got the kids, and by all accounts has a string of boyfriends, certainly an active and fulfilling sex life. And what's he got? What's he worked his arse off for, for the best part of two decades?

With all this in mind, he said fuck it to himself. Fuck it. And he rolled out of his hot, damp, stinking bed, determined to do something about it. Despite the hour.

He was going to go cruising, whether people went cruising in Las Gaviotas or not. What else could he do?

Skipping the buffet breakfast, suddenly extremely eager to get out there and on with it, Mark found himself on the narrow promenade studded with chewing gum, beyond the street in front of the hotel. There were a few palm trees but more rubbish bins, except most people seemed to have missed those, and there was litter – half-crushed beer and Coke cans and fast-food wrappers and cartons – all over the place.

There weren't many people about, however. Or rather

there were, but they were either small kids or very obviously the parents of small kids.

Nothing had opened yet. The cafés and bars and tourist shops were shut and shuttered.

It was one of the most cheap and depressing places Mark had ever been to, despite the fact that it was so hot and sunny. Though, actually, Mark quickly found it was too hot already. And though it was sunny, it was very muggy and slightly hazy, as if, somewhere not so far off out in the Mediterranean, a storm was brewing.

He was wearing just his Speedos, a red singlet top and a pair of off-road sandals. He was carrying some money, his room keys and a condom, in a waterproof tube, which hung around his neck on a metal chain. He bought this when he was in Thailand last year. He found it indispensable. There is enough room for money, room keys, depending on the ring, and four condoms at a squeeze. But today, at this hour, he thought one condom would be enough.

Mark was hoping that things might be more promising once the promenade and shops end, and the sandy scrub and half-built hotels and villas begin. Las Gaviotas was still expanding, though clearly on a shoestring.

But stepping off the promenade and on to a dusty path that ran beside the beach, the place suddenly seemed even more deserted. Mark had hoped, he realised, that there might at least be the odd builder who fancied a break from building and a piece of male arse. However, it being August, he supposed that that was being overly optimistic. It was too hot for building anything. Way too hot for manual labour.

Actually, what he was really hoping was that beyond the shops and promenade there would be a nudist bit and beyond the nudist bit a gay nudist bit. There would be if this were France, he thought. But being Spain, and stuffed full of English, there didn't appear to be anything of the sort.

Just more half-built buildings, and scrub, and dirty sand.

This far from the centre of Las Gaviotas, they clearly didn't bother to clean the sand, not that they made much of an effort closer in.

Still, Mark walked on, now on the scruffy beach itself, hoping anyone really might materialise. It was so hot that he had to take off his top. He wanted to take off his sandals too, because they were making his feet sweat terribly, but the sand was too hot for bare feet.

He wanted to take off his Speedos also, but that was clearly not done here.

He was becoming tired and short of breath, yet the beach and signs of construction went on, except still there was virtually no sign of human life. Not an inkling of a nudist scene, let alone a gay nudist cruising scene.

Then he had a brain wave. He was here for another four days. He knew he would die of loneliness before then. Of sexual frustration at the very least. If nothing was to change. If he didn't at least attempt to do something about it.

His brain wave – he would invent a gay nudist cruising scene. Far away from the centre of Las Gaviotas, and the kiddies and cafés and karaoke bars, beyond most of the rest of half-built Las Gaviotas, would be where like-minded individuals, or groups for all he cared, in fact even better if there were groups – as long as they weren't mutually exclusive – came for some mutual relief, and proud showing off of all their physical assets.

He would invent the scene right now.

And so he stepped out of his Speedos and rolled them up inside his singlet, leaving him starkers except for his chunky sandals and his money tube, which, of course, had another purpose beyond just looking after his money.

It felt good to be naked in the hot muggy air, the sun on his large, bald body – ever since he'd taken to shaving his head he had also taken to shaving his chest and pubic region, though he just snips at the hair on his balls with a pair of nail scissors.

He's not into shaving his scrotum – he did try once, but never again.

With his free hand he felt his nearly hairless balls, cupping the weight, before gently massaging them with his fingers. He moved on to his penis, which, ever since he'd been Speedoless, had swollen to a semi-erect state. But even when it was fully erect nowadays, he could no longer make it as hard as he once could. He pulled his foreskin back and forth briefly, to see how it felt, out in the open, in ever-more-boiling heat.

At first he could feel the air where his foreskin had been, then it quickly became indistinguishable, as the end of his penis became wet and sticky and very warm indeed, and the rest of his penis became a little more erect. He walked over to the shoreline. His Speedos and rolled-up singlet in one hand, his penis in the other.

He thought of Jacques, as he so often did when he masturbated. Jacques' firm, muscly thighs, and tight, hairy buttocks. Despite always looking impeccable and wearing exquisite clothes, Jacques did not believe in shaving his body hair. And being French, from, originally, the Mediterranean – of all places, Mark thought – he was especially hairy.

Mark's mind pictured Jacques lying on his front, his firm hairy thighs slightly spread, his hairy buttocks ripe and ready. This is the image Mark focuses on when he's masturbating and about to come. He actually pictures himself coming, spraying Jacques' thighs and buttocks, a large dollop landing between Jacques' bum, which then starts to slide ever further between Jacques' buttocks, and feeling it sliding down there Jacques helpfully lifts his arse in the air a little, and spreads his thighs a little too, and Mark puts his free hand between Jacques' thighs, between his buttocks, and massages his come into Jacques' arsehole, with first his forefinger, then second finger, then third and fourth, and then his thumb, until he has his whole hand in there, which he works deeper, his own come providing the lubricant, until he's fisting Jacques.

Mark imagines all this just before he comes. Usually he comes well before he's actually fisting Jacques. When he's only a couple of fingers in.

But not this morning. Ankle deep in the Med, furiously pumping away, Mark was seeing in his mind what he usually sees, after he comes, when he was suddenly aware of someone on the beach, a hundred yards or so up the shoreline.

In fact, he realised that he was probably aware of them subconsciously a little before that, which was why he hadn't come with his usual speed.

He stopped what he was doing, unsure as to whether they had seen anything or not. They were so far away, yet he could make out it was a man, with a beard, in a white shirt or T-shirt. He was walking just in the water, with the sun behind him, which blurred everything, so from where Mark was he almost looked as if he were walking on water.

Mark didn't know what to do. Part of him thought that this could be the answer to his dreams. Perhaps the man had been spying on him from somewhere, seen what he was doing and decided to join in the fun. Though Mark also thought, dressed like that he could be some sort of official, and was on his way to berate Mark. Or worse. Arrest him.

Not willing to chance it, despite desperately wishing it were some nice young man, eager to help relieve him – there can be nothing more frustrating, Mark thought, than being on the verge of coming and having to stop – Mark decided to turn the other way and walk quickly back to Las Gaviotas.

He also decided to pull his Speedos back on. However, not wanting to make this too obvious he managed to sort of step into them as he walked. Turning around, he saw that the man was still following him. Indeed, the man was closing ground.

Back in his Speedos Mark felt a little safer. That no one could possibly think he'd been doing anything wrong or obscene. However, he still didn't want the man to think that he had been doing something wrong, and had suddenly decided to put his trunks back on. Nor did he want the man – if he'd been after something else – to get the wrong idea about him.

It was a terrible quandary, in the ferocious heat and glare, with the hazy sun bouncing off the sea. Was he missing a wonderful opportunity or about to be in serious trouble? Or neither?

And on top of everything, his penis, tucked inside his Speedos, was still semi-erect, and he just felt so fucking randy, and he knew he had to do something about that pretty soon.

Not wanting to make it look too obvious – with the more solid structures of Las Gaviotas materialising to his right, and small crowds of people coming well into view – Mark found himself trying to make his Speedos as tiny as possible. So the man following him wouldn't think he had been shamed into getting dressed – because he had been doing something he shouldn't have been doing – or that he wasn't in the market for some fun, if that was on offer. Which, turning around for about the tenth time, he thought might be a distinct possibility. He didn't look too official. Just dressed in a white shirt, and bearded.

Mark found it surprisingly easy to adjust the cover of his Speedos. Though he was still holding his red singlet, he managed to roll the waistband down a couple of inches, and rather than try to roll up the legs he pushed the sides in, into the crack of his arse, where they seemed to stay quite happily. It was probably made easier because his trunks were pretty old and had seen at least two holidays in Thailand. And his arse was so large and flabby, and his trunks had only been badly stretched over it before.

I've thonged my Speedos, he thought with a chuckle, as he started to walk between groups of people and past a row of beached pedalos – the man with the white shirt and beard closing ground still.

Maybe there's some money in this, it occurred to Mark – ever the venture capitalist. Trunks you can thong at the drop of a hat.

The Balcony

'That man's following him,' says Alicia.

'Who?' says Mikey.

'That guy in a white shirt. With a beard,' says Alicia.

'You're kidding,' says Mikey. 'Maybe not.' There is a guy in a white shirt, with a beard, who does seem to be following what's-his-name. They are beyond the pedalos and appear to be heading towards their hotel.

'What do you think they are up to?' says Alicia.

'What do you reckon?'

'I don't know,' she says.

'I don't think it takes much imagination,' he says, hanging further over the balcony to get a better look, as the two men cross the road – the fat one in a thong just ahead of the Jesus lookalike. 'The dirty wankers.'

'At this hour?' says Alicia. 'It's not even 10.'

'That hasn't stopped us before,' he says. 'Come here, babe.'

'Hey, mind my make-up,' Alicia says, as Mikey grabs her, pulls her into him and starts kissing her on the neck, his wet rough tongue grazing her soft skin. 'Hey,' she says, feeling Mikey's hands tug at the ties on her bikini. Feeling his erection press into her abdomen. The thing about Mikey, Alicia has long been aware, and invariably enjoyed, is his ability to get an erection at a moment's notice.

Mikey gets Alicia's bikini bottom undone in about half a second. He fucking loves string bikinis. Who the hell invented them? he's thinking. Deserves a fucking medal. An OBE. A knighthood. A lot of fucking money.

What's more, he can feel what appears to be a very neatly trimmed bush. Alicia's?

Pushing Alicia away a bit, so he can get a better look, he says, 'What's happened here? Change of heart?' He can't believe he didn't notice this yesterday, or the day before, realising he probably hasn't seen Alicia properly naked for days. But he was whacked, from having to sort out his work, from all the preparation for going away, from having to say goodbye to his mates at the Giraffe, which was a little more exhausting, and sexually draining, than he had anticipated, and then having to get up so early for their flight.

Having been so whacked, he hasn't noticed until now that Alicia has finally trimmed her bush. Properly.

He has his hands all over her vagina, cupping it, stroking it, loving it. He gets on his knees, on the balcony, pushes Alicia gently up against the low concrete balcony wall, and immediately starts performing cunnilingus.

'I always do this when I go on holiday,' she says, thinking it's not like the first time I've had such a wax and a trim, though she went to a new place, in West Norwood – she wasn't going to go to Wendy's again – and they probably took off more than usual. She hadn't thought anything much about it, until now. Apart from perhaps the fact that she'd gone to the effort and Mikey hadn't even noticed it.

And, if she's being honest, she did do it for him as much as she did it because she was going on holiday and knew she would be wandering around in her new string bikini, which is completely white and would show up the tiniest little pube.

She did it for Mikey because she's still feeling guilty about what happened, with Karl the Ozzie supply teacher, on the last day of term. She doesn't know why she should be feeling guilty, having a fucking good idea what Mikey's been up to these past months at the Giraffe, but she does.

Or rather she knows that this holiday is the make or break of their relationship. She's not making any more effort after this. This is it. She's giving him one more chance. What's more, she has thought and still thinks, she'll put everything she has into it.

She doesn't mind Mikey going down on her, but it's not her favourite thing. He's a little too vigorous with his tongue. Either he presses it too hard against her clit or he tries to stick it too far into her, meaning that his nose is then pressing too hard against her pubic bone. Either way it's pretty uncomfortable, and she hardly ever comes that way. What she likes best is screwing him, with him on top, boring as that is, she knows. But it works for her, as long as he doesn't go at it too fast.

She likes Mikey to take his time, and be a little gentle. She likes it best when rather than just concentrating on actually fucking her, he sort of grinds into her. He's quite good at it, if he remembers exactly how.

Mikey, of course, likes screwing her from behind. He likes it best when she's on the bed, on all fours, her arse poking right up. He likes to trail his cock up and down her arse crack, dipping it into her vag and out again – teasing her, so he thinks – and along the full length of her arse crack, and against her arsehole, and finally back into her vag, which is when he really likes to go at it. With his mind thinking about the girls at the Giraffe, and the most recent porn he's seen on the box.

Sometimes he's had Alicia on the bed, on all fours, backed right up to the bottom of the bed, and he's given her one while he's been standing. He finds he can get more thrust that way, rather than if he's kneeling too. Also, he likes to put his hands on her buttocks, and sort of prise them apart while he's at it, so he gets a good look at exactly what's going on down there. At his glistening cock sliding in and out of her, and her arsehole all wrinkly and brown, and so tiny looking.

Sometimes he's had Alicia while she's standing too. Once he had her while she was cleaning her teeth, in the bathroom. She was hanging on to the sink. He just walked in, started kissing her neck, and the next thing he knew he had his hands up her nightie, and was playing with her, making her wet, and he just bent her over the sink, lifted up her nightie some more, and slid in. It was all over in a couple of minutes, if that.

He once had her out in the country too. They had had lunch in a pub, drank too much to drive anywhere, so they decided to go for a walk to walk it off. Mikey always feels particularly randy after a few at lunchtime, and this was no exception.

They hadn't got far, down a muddy, overgrown lane, when they started kissing and groping each other. And soon they knew they had to do it. At least Mikey did. He wanted to do it more than anything, sod being spotted by a passer-by. But the ground was too wet to lie on, and there were brambles and stuff either side of the lane, too thick to wander through.

The lane went on and on, and Mikey's sexual frustration grew and grew – Alicia kept putting her hand down his jeans, giving him a fiddle, then licking her fingers, making a show of it. And he kept putting his hands up her skirt, getting his fingers inside her knickers and inside her, loving how wet she was, and how wet she was making her knickers. The feel of damp knicker fabric has always been a huge turn-on, he has found.

Then they came to a stile, and before Alicia had clambered over, when she had just put her hands on the top bar, Mikey lifted her skirt all the way up and pressed his groin into her arse, and mock pumped her, which gave him the idea of doing it for real.

The mock pumping became real when Alicia bent over more and reached around for the fly of his jeans, but Mikey knew he'd be quicker, and pushed her hand away, getting his cock out himself, and with Alicia bent over, her hands on the top bar, and with her skirt already halfway up her back, all he had to do was tug her knickers down a little, and because she was so wet, he pushed straight in.

And because they were in the middle of the countryside, at a stile, on a marked footpath, he thought they had better be quick. Besides, he was bursting. Doing it out in the open, where they might be caught, only added to the excitement. As he pumped away, Alicia let go of the bar with one hand, reached under and started to play with herself, obviously excited too. Mikey came before Alicia, well before. Afterwards, when they had readjusted their clothes and made themselves look respectable, she said she had come too, but Mikey wasn't at all sure she had come. Not that it bothered him too much, but he likes it when she moans.

Climbing over the stile, to continue their walk, Mikey noticed a dollop of spunk on the bottom plank, which must have got there when he pulled out. At that angle, and having been in so deep, and having gone at it with such vigour, there was a definite sucking sound and then a plop, as he pulled out – some spunk obviously coming out with him and landing on the bottom rung of the stile.

It was one of the most memorable fucks of his life – out in the open, with the possibility of being seen – which gives him an idea.

Alicia thinks, I know what's coming now.

Mikey stops lapping at her fanny, stands, twizzles her around and pushes her back up against the balcony wall, so she's facing the sea this time, and Mikey's pressing her from behind.

She's still wearing her bikini top, so for anyone looking up from the beach, all they'd see would be her top half, with Mikey close behind her. She sees how crowded the beach has suddenly got. All the sun loungers are occupied. People, children, are playing on what beach there is left, and paddling and swimming. There are inflatables and balls everywhere. And a plane is flying across the bay towing a banner that says CLUB TROPICANA.

She feels his erection in his shorts, and she feels Mikey crouching a little so he can line his erection up with the bottom of her bottom. She stands away from the balcony a bit, so she can bend over slightly, and before she has time to free Mikey's cock he's done it himself, dropping his shorts to his feet, and she's got his bare, erect cock prodding her behind, hard.

She knows that if anyone had a pair of binoculars, or were looking up from the beach carefully, they'd probably be able to work out what was going on, but the balcony was really quite private. There were full-length screens at either end, and unless the person above was hanging right over it would be hard for any hotel guests to have a clue.

She has to bend over a little more to accommodate Mikey's cock. But because he had been lapping away, she was sodden already, and it sank in no problem. Now it's there she feels rather pleased about it, and pushes back on him, really beginning to enjoy herself. Knowing that if they keep at it, and if she can take a hand off the ledge and continue to balance comfortably, and masturbate all at the same time, she might well come, for the first time ever out in the open air.

She thinks the heat must have something to do with it. How you become so slippery with sweat so quickly.

'Look,' grunts Mikey, over Alicia's shoulder, 'there. That's him.'

'Where, who?' Alicia says. She's freed a hand and has begun to masturbate, frantically, feeling the shaft of Mikey's cock push in and out of her with her fingertips, sensing Mikey's not going to last too long. The beach is a sandy-coloured blur, the sea a pale-blue blur, the palm trees a wave of green and brown.

'It's him, the Jesus lookalike, looking like he's had a right arseful. Look at the way he's walking.'

Alicia is not sure where to look. She's not sure she's bothered. She hates it when Mikey's homophobic. Thinks it's more than a little rich too, given his obsession with arseholes.

'And there's what's-his-name following.' Mikey is desperately short of breath, but he doesn't let up on the rhythm. 'No, look. They're talking. Something's definitely gone on. Fuck, they were quick. A lot quicker than us.'

Alicia stops masturbating. She's rapidly losing interest in Mikey shagging her from behind. 'That's because they're blokes,' she says, seeing Mark – his name has come to her – and the other guy, the Jesus lookalike, walk across the road and on to the promenade. 'As long as they shoot their load, what do they care?' She feels Mikey come, his penis working like a little pump, feels him shudder. 'See,' she says. His cock is shrinking inside her. 'What did I say? Now what are you going to do?'

'Go down to the beach?' says Mikey. 'Go for a swim?' He laughs, catching his breath. 'Watch you finish off?'

'Like fuck you are,' she says.

Rent a Car

Now she realises why she hardly ever sees the rest of her family. She hates them. Her father is a sexist, bigoted pig, and a moron. Her mother is an idiot, for sticking with him. Her sister Sally has completely lost it. Brian, her husband, never had it.

Her half-sisters, Alicia, a so-called teacher, and Zara, a rep, of all illustrious things, are total slappers. They are both quite pretty, especially Alicia – Zara's too short – which makes Catherine hate them even more.

Their mother Janet – Catherine still can't believe she's here too – is just silly. Catherine almost feels sorry for her, but she's too quiet and timid and pathetic to conjure up any real feelings of sympathy. She thinks the woman should have been put out of her misery years ago.

As for Mark, Catherine finds him more repulsive every time she sees him. He's so fat and bald, and sunburned, and bent. She couldn't help laughing when she saw him on the beach yesterday. In his trunks, which were very clearly at least three sizes too small, and one of those singlet tops, which was far too tight as well. He looked more like a yob than a raging queen.

She can't believe she was once married to him. It must have been for the money. She can't possibly think there were any other reasons.

God, Catherine is cross this morning. She's sick of everybody already. Why she let herself be persuaded to come on this bloody so-called holiday, in such a sham of a hotel, organised by her tarty little half-sister, she'll never know. She hates her father. Why would she want to come all the way to Majorca for his bloody birthday? And what a ludicrous idea the whole thing is, anyway. A party, in Majorca, for Dad's seventieth, with all the family. Every bloody one of them.

Well, he wasn't going to get any friends to come all this way. He doesn't have any friends.

Thinking about it, she can see it wasn't quite such a ludicrous idea for her father and her mother to have come up with – even if he is supposed to be chronically ill with heart disease, and thinks this could well be the last chance to get everybody together before he finally, thankfully croaks. It was obviously designed so the two of them could have a free holiday. They have always been the most chronic freeloaders.

Catherine doesn't want to be here. She can't bear it.

'It'll be nice for your children,' her mother had said.

So what, Catherine felt like saying back. She doesn't like her children. Jack, Toby and Victoria, three really horrible kids, she wouldn't wish on anybody. They all take after their father.

Well, he can have them today, she thinks. All fucking day too. Because she's going to do something different.

As much as she's sick of being stuck in the same foul hotel with all her family, she's just as sick of squeezing herself into a bikini, lying on the joke of a beach out front and wishing she were somewhere else.

Today she's going to escape – her family, the compound, her sad, desperate life.

She's going on an adventure. Fuck them all.

Fuck it, she says to herself. It's nearly lunchtime and she's only made it to Alcudia. She had to wait for ever for the bus. She doesn't know what she's doing at her age having to get a bus, anyway. But it was the only way she could get out of Las Gaviotas. The people behind the desk at the hotel convinced her it was quick and easy, that everyone did it all the time. 'There's a shuttle,' one of the reps told her – not her tarty little half-sister but a fat monster of a girl.

She should have known better.

What's more, Catherine realises, she got off the fucking bus too early. Not that she could have stayed on it a moment longer. Shuttle, my arse. Apart from stopping every hundred yards or so, picking up more and more people, it wasn't even air-conditioned. It stank. Body odour, smelly feet, cheap suntan lotion, sweets, soiled nappies, old peasants.

It made Catherine gag. Now she's God knows where on the outskirts of Alcudia. She had been led to believe that the town was rather pretty and had a very old, part-medieval centre. Not from what she's seen of it.

She's on a dusty, deserted street. There are no shops, no people, not even any moving cars, and no shade whatsoever. The sun is almost directly overhead. It's so hot that Catherine thinks she might faint.

Plus, she's not dressed for the weather. So desperate to get out of the hotel and away from her dreadful family she forgot her sunhat. She put on her white-denim skirt, which is far too thick, and already filthy from the bus, her appliquéd Monsoon T-shirt, which is both too delicate and too clingy, the wrong sandals, and underneath all this her bikini. Which was always too tight and too hot, made from some appalling man-made fibre which doesn't so much breathe as suffocate.

Nor does it stretch. It just seems to get tighter and tighter. An ever-shrinking bikini.

Her tits are great, saggy lumps of sweat, crammed into some medieval contraption – that's the only medieval thing around here, she thinks. And they hurt, especially where the material is rubbing against her chest, as they flop up and down as she struggles to make headway on the deserted street.

Where the fuck is everybody, she keeps thinking. She's still seen no one. At work? She didn't think the Spanish did a lot of work. On the beach? Are they all on the beach?

For the first time she's been here she wishes she were on the beach too. Slipping out of her horrible clothes and into the cool sea. Except she's fully aware that even the sea is not exactly cool around here. It's too hot, like everything else.

Worse than her tits is what's going on between her legs. Her fanny feels impossibly hot and clammy and itchy; she can't fucking bear it. 'I can't fucking bear it,' she shouts, wanting to cry. 'Fuck it, fuck it, fuck it.'

Stopping by a dusty, low wall, checking no one is about, Catherine puts her bag down on the ground, reaches under her skirt with both hands and pulls down and steps out of her bikini bottoms. The relief is immediate. Although it is not exactly cool air that she suddenly feels between her legs, it's not unbearably constricting or suffocating or itchy either. It is fresh air of a sort.

She stuffs her bikini bottoms into her bag, half thinking she'd like to throw them away, and resumes her lonely walk through the deserted streets of Alcudia.

Parched, faint, fucked, Catherine knows she can't go on much further. She still hasn't seen anyone, at least anyone who wasn't some form of village idiot or itinerant youth on a moped. But in the distance she thinks she can see a red and white sign. She immediately takes this to be a café, or a bar, or a restaurant.

She's not going to start thinking about how awful her little adventure is turning out to be. For the moment she's going to concentrate on getting to this establishment and having a drink, and maybe something to eat, and getting them to order her a taxi to take her to somewhere decent.

'Fuck,' she says, slowly closing in on the sign. 'It fucking can't be.'

The closer she gets, the more apparent it becomes that the tatty red and white sign is not advertising a café, or a bar, or a restaurant. It says, AUTOS SERRA RENT A CAR.

Her sandals are killing her. Though they are excruciatingly tight, her feet are still slipping around in them because they are so sweaty. And fat. And no doubt stink.

'Fucking rent a car,' she says. 'Who the fuck needs that?' But maybe, she thinks, she'll be able to get a glass of water, at least, in the office. They must have one of those water cooler things.

Maybe, she also thinks, approaching the door, if the fucking place is open, she could hire a car and drive off to somewhere decent. But she doesn't want to hire a car. She doesn't want to have to think about driving on the wrong side of the road, in a nasty little Spanish hire car, and then have to think about where the hell she's going. She wants to be driven somewhere – to a wonderful, secluded, five-star hotel, with a beautiful outdoor terrace and pool, and the most fantastic Michelin-starred restaurant, and gorgeous, sophisticated, unattached men wandering about the place. La Residencia, that's where she wants to be. The best hotel in Majorca. The place Mark used to go on about, not that he ever took her there. Where, supposedly, Princess Di used to go on holiday to get away from everything. Well, Catherine wants to get away from everything. Her family are just as awful as the bloody Royal Family. And why shouldn't she do it in style, in luxury?

Amazingly, Autos Serra rent a car is open. The door to the

office works. Catherine doubts whether there is anybody inside, at least anybody remotely normal. But all she really cares is whether there is a water cooler, and a plastic cup of chilled acqua.

The office smells musty, damp. But it is cool, air-conditioned. The shock almost makes Catherine shiver. But it's a delightful shock, and in the cool air she senses how hot she really was and just how wet with sweat she is. She looks down at her chest, the way her overpriced, undersized Monsoon top clings to her like a wet T-shirt, like she just climbed out of a pool with it on. Or she was in one of those awful wet T-shirt competitions. Every line, every seam of her bikini top stands out. And her nipples do also, obviously reacting to the sudden drop in temperature.

She hates her tits. And she hates Monsoon. Normally, everything from Monsoon is enormous. For some reason her top isn't. Or maybe her tits have grown recently. Maybe she's pregnant. At forty-three. But it would have had to have been an immaculate conception. Unless the estate agent she bonked the other week – she can't even remember his name – was using a dodgy condom. Or the condom didn't fit very well, which wouldn't have surprised her because he had a tiny penis. One of the smallest she's ever come across. Really.

No bell or anything sounded when she stepped inside the Autos Serra office, and still no one has appeared.

She's beginning to worry whether it is closed but they have forgotten to lock up. She hasn't completely cooled off yet and she looks about for a water cooler.

'Thank fucking God,' she says. In the corner, by a dusty plant, is a water cooler, over half full. There are plenty of plastic cups newly stacked where they should be too. She helps herself to a cup, drinks it in one, refills it and takes it over to a bench and sits down. Once, she can see, someone made an effort with the décor of the place, but that must have been many years ago.

She didn't realise how much her limbs ache, and her feet. She kicks off her sandals and spreads out, feeling the cool air on her feet and her legs, and between her legs. Because it feels so good and she's sure no one is about, she pushes her heavy skirt up further to expose more of her skin to the chilled air. And because her thighs are not as slim as they used to be she parts her legs more to aid the passage of air to right between her legs and her still-burning fanny. It always takes ages for her to cool down properly – after tennis, for instance. Or after shopping. Or, she laughs to herself, because she's feeling so much happier about everything, after shagging.

However, she's utterly exhausted and when a man appears behind the counter she can't be bothered to move an inch.

'Hola,' Pedro says. He was in his office, on the net, watching a webcam surreptitiously set up in a women's public toilet in Iceland. The camera must have been placed somewhere near the bottom of the door, pointing slightly up and straight at the toilet. It's the best-placed webcam he's ever seen.

He likes the Scandinavian look. The way these women are so big and healthy looking, and fair, yet hairy. He likes the way they are so natural. He wants to go to Iceland.

'Oh hi,' Catherine says, not moving. She realises she must have been on the verge of drifting off, if in fact she hadn't drifted off, sitting there. Slowly a man comes into focus. A typical Spanish-looking man – short, dark and shifty-looking. Though he has a certain something. She can tell that already.

Pedro can't believe what he's seeing. He didn't notice immediately, but the woman sitting in his office is not wearing any knickers. He can't stop looking at her crotch, but it is not his fault. Her skirt is so short, and she's not exactly crossing her legs or making any attempt to cover up her most intimate parts.

He simply can't believe it. There he was, looking at live pussy on the internet, and now he's looking at the real thing in his office. Also, the woman looks vaguely familiar. He wonders where he's seen her before.

'I help?' he says.

'Yes,' Catherine says. But her mind is not working very clearly. All she can think is that she's meant to be having an adventure, on her own, away from her family. And she's in some strange office, with a shifty Spaniard, who's looking at her in a very lechy way.

The thing Pedro likes about older women, and Scandinavian women in particular, is that they don't all shave their pussies. He likes hair where it should be. He likes the natural look. As long as they are not too hairy and dark. That's the problem he has with Mediterranean women, and Zara his girlfriend. They are too hairy, or in Zara's case too bald. This woman seems to be just right. He likes the light shade of brown her pubes are.

He still can't believe she's sitting there, in his office like that. She is a gift from God, he thinks.

'How do I get out of here?' she says. 'And to somewhere nice? I want to go to La Residencia. That's where I want to go. How do I get there?'

'You want to hire a car?' Pedro says.

'No,' she says, increasingly disconcerted by the way he's looking at her. Though also a little intrigued. He seems to be staring at her crotch. It comes to her. Not only is her skirt halfway up her thighs, not only is she sitting in a rather indelicate way, but she is not wearing any knickers. Her bikini bottoms are stuffed in her bag. But not wanting to draw any more attention to her state of undress, she resists either pulling her skirt down or crossing her legs. While he's looking at her so intently, she knows she'll have to just ride it out.

Occasionally, she has gone knickerless, but mostly it was on purpose, when she was wanting to feel risqué, or more particularly when she was wanting whoever to know that she was teasing them. Never before has she found herself in such a situation by accident. She feels a small thrill, and wonders if her adventure has just begun.

Pedro looks away, at a faded map of Majorca behind the desk, and back. Even though he took his eyes off her, Catherine did not move. Also, despite the cooling breeze of the air-conditioning floating between her legs, it suddenly feels warm and tingly down there. You are so rude, she says to herself.

'This is not a taxi,' Pedro says. 'This is rent a car.'

'I don't want to drive,' Catherine says.

Pedro walks out from behind the counter. He wants to get a better look. He wants to see just how real and natural this woman is. He wants to get close enough to smell her. His mind has been full of pictures, of images, today. He wants smell now. Followed by touch.

Also, he wants her to see that he is something of a man too. He has always been proud of his physique. The fact that for a Spaniard he is not so short. Plus, he's proud of his chest, and how trim and in shape he is, for a thirty-eight-year-old – at least, that's how old he tells people he is. He plays table football whenever he can.

He has an erection. He knows how obvious it must look, stuffed inside his thin, dark-blue Autos Serra office trousers. Zara is always teasing him about it, when she teases him.

If he wasn't so skinny, Catherine is thinking, she'd fancy him. As it is, she's not entirely uninterested, especially as he seems to have a rather significant bulge in his trousers. Things are definitely looking up, she tells herself.

'Do you want me to drive?' Pedro says. 'I go that way.' He doesn't. It's almost on the opposite side of the island from his home, over the quiet Serra de Tramuntana mountains. An hour's drive at least.

'That's a good idea,' she says, standing at last, walking towards the door, keen to get going, feeling a trickle of something slide down her inner thigh, wondering whether there is a wet stain on the back of her skirt – a stain of sweat, or excited fanny juice – wondering whether she should pop to the loo and slip on her bikini bottoms before the journey.

No, she decides. What would be the point? They'll be round her ankles before long. So she hopes.

Fucked

Janet didn't bring the Rabbit. She didn't bring the Robo Cock, either. She just brought herself, and one decent outfit, and the idea that she should try to be as pleasant and friendly as possible. She's not thinking about sex or past relationships. She's too old to cause a scene. Charlie's too ill. And it is certainly not the occasion, anyway. In fact, she was flattered to be asked. In a way it seems to her like everything has been moving towards this point for years, for decades. It feels both like some sort of closure and a new beginning. At fifty-eight she can't argue with that.

She's in her hotel room, getting ready for the big event. Her outfit is from Whistles, a dark-red linen skirt and matching top. Her underwear is from Janet Reger – the knickers are all front and no back – not because she has any intention of showing them off, but it's her silent homage to Charlie. She knows he would appreciate the gesture. And, well, she's not going to even think about it, because that's not why she's here. Truly.

The party starts in twenty minutes. She's much more excited and nervous than she thought she would be.

*

'Wow,' says Brian. 'I was wondering when you were going to finally put that stuff on.'

Sally emerges from the bathroom in just her make-up and Truly You underwear. It's the first time she's put on both the bra and the thong at the same time. She feels surprisingly good in them. The rash from her bikini wax has died down, and having spent the last five days on the beach, sunbathing and swimming, she feels brown and in better shape than she's been in for years. She actually feels sexy.

Brian's on the balcony, in his black trousers and white short-sleeved shirt. Sally thinks he looks like a policeman with a beer gut. He's drinking yet another San Miguel. He moves over to the door. 'You don't think we've got time for a quick one?'

'No, Brian, I don't think we've got time for a quick one,' Sally says. She goes to the cupboard where her dress has been hanging ever since they arrived. It's a very simple summer dress, in cream, from Joseph. It's not just see-through in the right light, but it clings to her so tightly that nothing is left to the imagination – every bit of her and her underwear. She slips it on, does the zip up herself – which is easy because it's on the side – walks into her shoes – a pair of low-heeled mules from M&S – and walks over to join her husband on the balcony.

'Ready,' she says, feeling the full force of the sultry evening heat. 'It's still bloody hot and sticky, isn't it?'

'Hey,' Brian says. 'Give us a kiss.' He has his hands on her arse and is trying to pull her into him. 'You look gorgeous.'

'Get your hands off me,' Sally says. 'You'll leave fat fingerprints all over my dress.' She wants to be pawed tonight, but not by Brian. She knows exactly whose hands she wants on her arse, and she's determined to give it her best shot. So much is crystallising in her head. The last few days have made her see things very clearly indeed. She feels useful, empowered.

She's on a mission.

'That's enough,' says Alicia, pushing Mikey away. He was sucking her right nipple, standing up, in the middle of the room, with his hand on her fanny, but on the outside of her underwear. She doesn't know why, but he always seems to suck her right nipple, not her left.

She wants to put her dress on. She wants his hands off her. She's been stuck in just her thong for what seems like hours, though she realises it's probably her fault for wearing such a provocative one. Plus, she did want to show it off a bit. She thinks it's hilarious and sexy at the same time.

Yes, she's in the black, diamanté Splendour. Amazingly, when she went back to Debenhams, they still had it. And it was in the sale. She got it for £8 instead of £15.

When Mikey first saw it on her, he said, 'Fuck me, Alicia, you look the real thing at last. A proper babe. Why have you been keeping this from me?'

'Why should I give you everything you want all the time?' she said.

'Yeah, but it's cruel,' Mikey said, 'to have denied me this for so long. I wouldn't have needed to keep going down the Giraffe had I known what was at home. Just kidding.'

Alicia is not wearing a bra tonight. Just the thong and her little black number, from Top Shop, but it looks posher than that, and a pair of stilettos. What could be simpler? she thinks. And what could be simpler than men?

She'll make do with Mikey for a bit longer, now she's got him exactly where she wants him.

'Mikey,' she says, totally on the spur of the moment and holding the back of her left hand in his face, 'what do you think I'm missing?'

*

Mark is the first one there. The space is empty except for a couple of bored-looking waiters behind the bar. But it looks quite pretty, Mark thinks, considering what a dump the hotel is. Clearly, the dark makes it all look better, and he likes the way the swimming pool is lit from underneath, and the way they have stuck proper flares around the gardens. The smell is the only problem. He noticed it the other day, but it seems worse tonight, perhaps because there is no breeze and it's so muggy.

Normally, the pool restaurant is open only during the day, but his ex-father-in-law, and his ex-father-in-law's illegitimate younger daughter, obviously pulled a few strings.

Mark realises he should probably be feeling a bit nervous about seeing Charlie, given how he treated Charlie's elder, and not illegitimate, daughter, but he's not nervous about that at all. If he is nervous, it's because he's not sure whether Jesus is going to show up, and if he does how it will go down.

But Mark didn't see why he shouldn't ask him – everyone else, except Catherine, he supposes, and maybe the woman Charlie had his illegitimate kids with, is bringing a partner. Why shouldn't he bring his new boyfriend? Apart from everything else, he really wants to see him again. He is wonderful. He loves everything about him – his body, his penis, especially that, even his beard. He's never been with a man with a beard before. It was a totally different experience – one of the best blow jobs he's ever had. And then when Jesus turned him over and buried his head between his buttocks and started tonguing him – it was so incredible it made him hard again almost immediately, and he means hard.

He hasn't fallen for someone quite like this since Jacques. It's made the trip already.

Mark walks over to the bar. It's been styled to look like a coconut. Or rather two halves of a coconut, with the bar bit in the middle. It seems a shame to have just a beer, in such a setting, so he asks for a piña colada.

Waiting for the boy to mix his drink he sees his ex-wife walk out of the hotel and along the path towards the pool area. He can't help feeling she's looking surprisingly good. She's trailed by their three children, all of whom appear to still be in their swimming costumes.

If it weren't for her horrible children, Catherine's thinking, she'd actually be looking forward to this evening. Not only that, she'd be looking forward to the rest of the holiday. It's turned out fabulously. For the first time in she doesn't know how long, she's met someone who's on her wavelength. A man of not many words, but someone with a lot of direction. And a very fat knob. It's the weirdest one she's ever seen. It's almost bulbous. But it's surprisingly effective.

She's asked Pedro tonight. She didn't see why she shouldn't. Everyone else is coupled up, except she supposes her ex-husband, and possibly Zara and Alicia's mother, that poor Janet woman. Why shouldn't she bring her new boyfriend?

She doesn't know whether he'll actually turn up. He seemed fine about the idea at first but when she described to him exactly where and when it was, and who would be there – not that that could possibly have made any difference, except for the presence of her ex-husband – he suddenly wasn't so keen. She thinks it must be because he knows all about the hotel, how it has this super-bug, or whatever it is, and also this sewage problem, and that any gathering held here is not exactly going to be the most spectacular.

But that's not the point, she thinks. She'll be here. And she has a little surprise for him. She's not wearing no underwear for once. Underneath her new frock, she's wearing her new Chantilly lace thong from Agent Provocateur. Ever since she nearly bought it weeks ago she'd been thinking about it. Finally, she had to go back. She bought the cream one, because her pubic hair is not particularly dark and she thought the colour would go better with her pale skin, though she's quite brown now.

However, and more important, it fits like a glove. It is easily the most comfortable thong she's ever worn. It is also the most expensive, which is probably why. She was staggered when she found out it cost £45, for such a tiny amount of material.

But right now she feels it was worth every penny. She feels fantastic. Fit, healthy, happy and sexy. Plus, she loves the fact that it's part of the Agent Provocateur Love line, because, as her daughter might say, she's loved up.

She's never had a holiday romance before, though she's determined to make up for lost time.

'You lot,' she says, turning around to her kids, 'why don't you disappear. Come back when your grandfather's here. Go on, piss off.'

'Mark,' she says, reaching the bar and her ex-husband, 'you look fucked.'

I want to hide. This is like the must embarrassing moment of my life.

You won't fucking believe it, but I've just seen Pedro and Jesus. What the fuck is Jesus doing here? It's bad enough that Pedro's here. I tried to put him off. Ever since he got back from Barcelona, I've been saying, don't come. My family are all nuts. You'll have a horrible time.

'I know I asked you ages ago,' I said to Pedro yesterday, on the phone, 'but I'm unasking you now.' The trouble is he probably didn't understand a word I was saying.

As for Jesus, I'm sure I didn't mention anything to him. Why would I have?

He must have come with Pedro. Except Pedro is talking to Catherine, my fat half-sister, though she's not looking too bad tonight – God knows what they are saying, unless she speaks Spanish, which wouldn't surprise me. And Jesus is talking to

Mark. Who's also fat, but gay. It's complicated, but Mark used to be married to Catherine, then he went off with a bloke called Jacques.

My family, I tell you, are really fucked up.

I shouldn't have shagged Jesus. I feel like such a slapper.

How could I have?

And I've gone to all this effort to look nice. I'm wearing my little black dress from H&M I wore the other night – not that I'm the only person here in a little black dress – and my fake Blahniks, not that anyone could spot that they were fake, and my best underwear, my nearly new Betrayal thong and bra from Knickerbox, and I've gone to loads of effort with my make-up for once, and I feel like I just want to disappear.

Oh no, here come Pedro and Catherine. I am so fucked.

Charlie says to Dorothy and Janet, 'We haven't done too badly between us, have we? Four lovely kids.'

As far as he can remember it's the first time all his children have been in the same place at the same time. And they don't look bad, especially the younger two in their little black dresses. But his older daughters, the ones he thinks of as his proper daughters, look all right as well, in their cream dresses. Better than he thinks they've both looked for ages.

But it's funny, he thinks, how different the two lots of them are. The one lot in cream, the other in black. He's always thought Catherine and Sally were so much more straight than Alicia and Zara. However, over the years he has learned how much appearances can deceive. Probably Catherine and Sally are the wild ones, and Alicia and Zara calm and rather chaste.

He's a proud man tonight. He might be fucked healthwise, but his brain is working as normal.

He just wishes his penis was. Neither Dorothy nor Janet is especially chaste. Janet is definitely not. He brought his beloved, and banned, little blue pills with him just in case, but he doesn't reckon he's going to get a chance to use them. He's barely seen Janet, not once on her own, anyway, and Dorothy's become awfully strict about what he puts in his mouth. He feels like it's the end of the road. He knew it was going to be like this, he supposes. But how he'd love to have one final, steamy bash at Janet's derrière. She's kept her looks, her figure, remarkably well. She could be half Dorothy's age, he thinks.

They are standing by the coconut, drinking cocktails. Charlie's not meant to drink alcohol, but it's his birthday, his seventieth, so of course he is having a cocktail, a JD and Coke. He got the waiter to top up his Coke with JD when Dorothy wasn't looking.

'They haven't always been lovely,' says Janet.

'No,' says Dorothy, 'and they can still be a right pain in the arse.'

I push Pedro in first. Then Jesus. This is why.

I see Pedro and Jesus chatting and looking at me and laughing – they've been doing this for hours, but stupid me still doesn't get it just yet. So I finally walk over to the both of them and say, 'What's the big joke?'

'You like men in beards?' Pedro says, laughing.

'I don't know what you mean,' I say.

Jesus says, 'Pedro, you like giving older women lifts?'

'What?' I say.

Pedro says, to Jesus, rubbing his head, 'You like the men with no hair? And big stomachs?'

They are both laughing in a very Spanish way. Then they start talking in Spanish, some private joke, except it's fast becoming a very public joke. I look around the immediate vicinity, and the first thing I see is Catherine, my fat, elder half-sister, mouthing something to Pedro and beckoning him over. I look in the other direction and Mark, Catherine's gay, fat ex-husband is winking at Jesus.

I look at Pedro and Jesus, who both smile at me in a very

mocking way, and sort of hunch their shoulders to say, sorry, that's the way it is. Which is when everything clicks, and I shove Pedro backwards into the pool. While Jesus is practically bent over double laughing, I push him in too.

And because I can't stand the embarrassment, and because I haven't exactly behaved brilliantly myself, I think what the fuck and jump in also.

Catherine goes in next. She's not sure what's quite gone on, or what has been said, or who pushed who first, but she thinks it's hilarious. Also she doesn't care how see-through her dress will look in the water or when she gets out, because she's fit and tanned and she's wearing her Love thong. Who's going to resist her in that? Not her Pedro.

It's partly because Alicia's had four piña coladas and two glasses of sangria, and partly because she can't see Mikey, and when Mikey's not about she always feels a little more confident, a little more wild. Also, she doesn't want to ruin her dress, so she kicks off her shoes, pulls her dress over her head, and makes sure everyone gets a good look at her, standing by the side of the pool in just her black diamanté thong, before she leaps in, thinking, maybe I don't want to marry Mikey, after all.

Brian can't believe his luck tonight. First he discovers his wife prancing about their hotel room in some seriously sexy gear, now he's watching his sisters-in-law and his half-sisters-in-law frolicking around a floodlit pool practically naked. It's the best thing he's seen for years. He doesn't know where Sally is, but right now he doesn't care. All he's concerned about is getting into that pool, and a handful of whatever first comes to hand.

Mark's got the bartender to make him a cosmopolitan, and because he's taking so much time and trouble over it he feels he can't just abandon him and jump in the pool with the others. As much as he doesn't want to let Jesus out of his sight

– the man is absolutely fucking gorgeous – the bartender is also rather cute. And if he's not mistaken he's as bent as he is.

Spotting her grandchildren approaching the pool area, Dorothy decides to head them off. She can't quite make out exactly what's going on in the pool right now, there is so much splashing and screaming, and wet clothes being flung everywhere, but if she knows her family it will not be very innocent. She leads the children back into the hotel, missing Sally and Mikey by a few seconds.

Sally and Mikey think they are heading for Sally's room, but they are not too bothered where they end up as long as it's somewhere private. Mikey doesn't normally go for older women, but there's something about Sally that he finds a huge turn-on. Perhaps it's just that she seems so keen, and also sort of naive. He couldn't believe it when she put her hand on his crotch by the bar and said to him, 'I'd love to see what's inside your trousers.' Mikey also thinks it's partly Alicia's fault that he's had to slip off with Sally. Alicia should have let him shag her in their hotel room before the party. She left him feeling so frustrated he would have fucked anything.

Charlie finds himself alone with Janet at last. They have wandered behind the coconut, well out of the view of everybody, and are walking towards the garden perimeter. They are holding hands, and Charlie says, 'What about for old times' sake?'

Janet laughs. 'I didn't think you were still capable.'

'What, me? I'll always be capable,' he says. He pats his shirt pocket, feeling for the Viagra pill he took the precaution of bringing from his room with him. What does he care if it's the last one he ever takes? He pops it in his mouth, pretending to cough.

'I've got a little surprise for you,' says Janet, tightening her grip on his hand. She can't believe she hasn't been so intimate with Charlie since Venice, all those years ago.

'Yes?' says Charlie. 'Don't tell me.' He swings her towards

him, quickly running his hands over her still surprisingly firm arse. 'I can guess,' he says. 'I can feel.' He starts to pull up her skirt, crumpling the linen as he goes.

Everything would be perfect, he thinks, if it wasn't for the smell. They must be near the rubbish bins. But he's not going to let that ruin the last bonk of his lifetime. Nothing is going to get in his way now.